Best Detective
Stories of
Agatha Christie

Full text edition

General Editors: Andy Hopkins and Jocelyn Potter

Addison Wesley Longman Limited
Edinburgh Gate, Harlow,
Essex CM20 2JE, England
and Associated Companies throughout the world.

The stories appearing in this volume have all been
previously published in the following books by
Agatha Christie: *Poirot Investigates, Poirot's Early Cases,*
The Listerdale Mystery, The Labours of Hercules
and *Miss Marple's Final Cases.*

© by Agatha Christie Limited

First published in the Bridge Series 1986
in association with Collims (Publishers) Limited
This edition first published in Longman Fiction 1996
Third impression 1998

ISBN 0 582 27523 7

Set in Adobe Granjon 10.5pt
Produced through Longman Malaysia, KPP

Acknowledgements

We are grateful to Addison Wesley Longman Limited
for permission to use in the Word List definitions
adapted from the third edition of the *Longman Dictionary*
of Contemporary English © Longman Group Limited (1995).

Cover photograph © Addison Wesley Longman Limited/Maggy Milner.
We are grateful to Trident Arms (antique weapons), Derby Road, Nottingham
for the loan of props.

Full text level books in the Longman Fiction series are unsimplified. They contain a full glossary
of words additional to the 3000-word vocabulary level of books at Advanced level.
Vocabulary level: 3000 words

Contents

Introduction

Agatha Christie is one of the most popular and best-known novelists ever, and her books have been translated into more languages than those of any other writer. Born Agatha Miller in the south-west of England, probably in 1891 (although the exact date is appropriately a mystery), she enjoyed a settled, comfortable childhood. Fred Miller, her American father, did not have to work for a living as he had a private income, and the family employed servants to help with the housework. Agatha later missed this easy way of life, which provided the background for many of her later stories.

Agatha was a quiet, imaginative child, and she used to amuse herself by making up stories in her head. Her mother did not believe that girls needed a formal education, and so she was not sent to school. She taught herself to read at a very early age. Her father taught her some mathematics and she learned to speak French extremely well from a young French girl who was employed in the household to do the family sewing. Her father died when she was eleven, and after his death the family was short of money, although they managed to keep on the family home, Ashfield, which the children loved.

During the First World War Agatha worked in a hospital, where she acquired the detailed knowledge of poisons which was very useful to her in later life! In 1914 she married Archibald Christie. They had a daughter, Rosalind, and the first years of the marriage were apparently happy. In 1926, however, came a great shock. Archie told her that he had fallen in love with another woman and wanted to leave her.

In the unhappy time that followed, a great mystery occurred. Agatha disappeared. Her car was found abandoned, and it was thought she might have killed herself or been murdered. Police asked for the help of thousands of people to search for her. Eventually, however, she was found safe in a hotel in the north of England. She appeared to have lost her memory, but the truth of the matter has never been discovered.

Agatha had always had a taste for adventure and after her marriage ended she decided to travel alone to the Middle East. She met a man called Max Mallowan, and they got married a year or two later. During the Second World War Agatha lived in London and again worked in a hospital. After the war her life continued to be happy and successful. She became very interested in the theatre and started to write plays as well as novels. She died in Wallingford, Oxfordshire, in 1976.

Agatha Christie wrote sixty-six detective novels in all, over a period of fifty-six years. Mainly set among the leisured classes, who live in large country houses, the books are famous for their clever story lines rather than the depth of characterisation.

Her first novel, *The Mysterious Affair at Styles*, is one of the best. *The Murder of Roger Ackroyd*, published in 1926, is famous in detective fiction for its surprising murderer. Some of her early stories seem very dated by their political perspectives, but many of her books have remained firm favourites over the years. The causes and morality of crime are discussed very little in the books, although these issues are touched on in *Murder on the Orient Express*. Other lasting favourites are *Why Didn't They Ask Evans?*, *Ten Little Niggers* and *And Then There Were None*. Under the name of Mary Westmacott, Agatha Christie wrote six light romantic novels. *Come, Tell Me How You Live* and *An Autobiography* are about her own life.

Several of Christie's stories were adapted for the stage. The most successful of these is *The Mousetrap*, the longest-running play in theatre history. Her stories have also been adapted for film, radio and television.

One secret of her success has been the creation of her detective heroes, often unlikely figures who have captured the imagination of the public. The first of these is perhaps the best known. Hercule Poirot is a Belgian private detective, a short man with a great love of order and enormous self-confidence, whose incomplete knowledge of the English language provides additional entertainment. To those around him, Poirot seems a figure of fun until he demonstrates the brilliance of his mind by finding another amazing solution to a seemingly impossible problem. Poirot features in Christie's first novel, and his fictional career continued over the years through many books to *Curtain* (1975), in which Poirot dies after investigating his last case.

Christie's other famous detective was another unlikely person to take on the role of detective. Miss Marple is at first sight a typical English unmarried elderly lady, totally involved in village life. She is gentle and conventional in appearance, but she is extremely interested in murder and she has the ability to solve the most horrible crimes. This contrast provides much dramatic potential, and television programmes based on the Miss Marple stories have made the character extremely popular. Other detective heroes created by Christie include Inspector Evans, a retired police officer, who features in one of these stories.

Agatha Christie wrote over 130 short stories. Seven of the best of these can be found in this collection. In many ways they are very different from each other but they are all great mysteries, with unexpected endings, that will challenge the reader.

The Mystery of Hunter's Lodge

"After all," murmured Poirot, "it is possible that I shall not die this time."

Coming from a convalescent influenza patient, I hailed the remark as showing a beneficial optimism. I myself had been the first sufferer from the disease. Poirot in his turn had gone down. He was now sitting up in bed, propped up with pillows, his head muffled in a woollen shawl, and was slowly sipping a particularly noxious *tisane* which I had prepared according to his directions. His eye rested with pleasure upon a neatly graduated row of medicine bottles which adorned the mantelpiece.

"Yes, yes," my little friend continued. "Once more shall I be myself again, the great Hercule Poirot, the terror of evildoers! Figure to yourself, *mon ami*, that I have a little paragraph to myself in *Society Gossip*. But yes! Here it is: 'Go it — criminals — all out! Hercule Poirot — and believe me, girls, he's some Hercules! — our own pet society detective can't get a grip on you. 'Cause why? 'Cause he's got *la grippe* himself'!"

I laughed.

"Good for you, Poirot. You are becoming quite a public character. And fortunately you haven't missed anything of particular interest during this time."

"That is true. The few cases I have had to decline did not fill me with any regret."

Our landlady stuck her head in at the door.

"There's a gentleman downstairs. Says he must see Monsieur Poirot or you, Captain. Seeing as he was in a great to-do — and with all that quite the gentleman — I brought up 'is card."

She handed me the bit of pasteboard. "Mr Roger Havering," I read.

Poirot motioned with his head towards the bookcase, and I obediently pulled forth *Who's Who.** Poirot took it from me and scanned the pages rapidly.

"Second son of fifth Baron Windsor. Married 1913 Zoe, fourth daughter of William Crabb."

"H'm!" I said. "I rather fancy that's the girl who used to act at the Frivolity — only she called herself Zoe Carrisbrook. I remember she married some young man about town just before the War."

"Would it interest you, Hastings, to go down and hear what our visitor's particular little trouble is? Make him all my excuses."

Roger Havering was a man of about forty, well set up and of smart appearance. His face, however, was haggard, and he was evidently labouring under great agitation.

"Captain Hastings? You are Monsieur Poirot's partner, I understand. It is imperative that he should come with me to Derbyshire today."

"I'm afraid that's impossible," I replied. "Poirot is ill in bed — influenza."

His face fell.

"Dear me, that is a great blow to me."

"The matter on which you want to consult him is serious?"

"My God, yes! My uncle, the best friend I have in the world, was foully murdered last night."

"Here in London?"

"No, in Derbyshire. I was in town and received a telegram from my wife this morning. Immediately upon its receipt I determined to come round and beg Monsieur Poirot to undertake the case."

"If you will excuse me a minute," I said, struck by a sudden idea.

I rushed upstairs, and in a few brief words acquainted Poirot with the situation. He took any further words out of my mouth.

"I see. I see. You want to go yourself, is it not so? Well, why not? You

---

**Who's Who*: a book that gives information about the lives of important British people should know my methods by now. All I ask is that you should report to me fully every day, and follow implicitly any instructions I may wire you."

To this I willingly agreed.

An hour later I was sitting opposite Mr Havering in a first-class carriage on the Midland Railway, speeding rapidly away from London.

"To begin with, Captain Hastings, you must understand that Hunter's Lodge, where we are going and where the tragedy took place, is only a small shooting box in the heart of the Derbyshire moors. Our real home is near Newmarket, and we usually rent a flat in town for the season. Hunter's Lodge is looked after by a housekeeper who is quite capable of doing all we need when we run down for an occasional weekend. Of course, during the shooting season, we take down some of our own servants from Newmarket. My uncle, Mr Harrington Pace (as you may know, my mother was a Miss Pace of New York), has, for the last three years, made his home with us. He never got on well with my father, or my elder brother, and I suspect that my being somewhat of a prodigal son myself rather increased than diminished his affection towards me. Of course I am a poor man, and my uncle was a rich one — in other words, he paid the piper! But, though exacting in many ways, he was not really hard to get on with, and we all three lived very harmoniously together. Two days ago, my uncle, rather wearied with some recent gaieties of ours in town, suggested that we should run down to Derbyshire for a day or two. My wife telegraphed to Mrs Middleton, the housekeeper, and we went down that same afternoon. Yesterday evening I was forced to return to town, but my wife and my uncle remained on. This morning I received this telegram." He handed it over to me:

COME AT ONCE UNCLE HARRINGTON MURDERED LAST NIGHT BRING GOOD DETECTIVE IF YOU CAN BUT DO COME — ZOE.

"Then, as yet you know no details?"

"No, I suppose it will be in the evening papers. Without doubt the police are in charge."

It was about three o'clock when we arrived at the little station of Elmer's Dale. From there a five-mile drive brought us to a small grey stone building in the midst of the rugged moors.

"A lonely place," I observed with a shiver.

Havering nodded.

"I shall try and get rid of it. I could never live here again."

We unlatched the gate and were walking up the narrow path to the oak door when a familiar figure emerged and came to meet us.

"Japp!" I ejaculated.

The Scotland Yard* inspector grinned at me in a friendly fashion before addressing my companion.

"Mr Havering, I think? I've been sent down from London to take charge of this case, and I'd like a word with you, if I may, sir.

"My wife——"

"I've seen your good lady, sir — and the housekeeper. I won't keep you a moment, but I am anxious to get back to the village now that I've seen all there is to see here."

"I know nothing as yet as to what——"

"Ex-actly," said Japp soothingly. "But there are just one or two little points I'd like your opinion about all the same. Captain Hastings here, he knows me, and he'll go on up to the house and tell them you're coming. What have you done with the little man, by the way, Captain Hastings?"

"He's ill in bed with influenza."

"Is he now? I'm sorry to hear that. Rather the case of the cart without the horse, your being here without him, isn't it?"

*Scotland Yard: the headquarters of the Criminal Investigation Department of London's police force

And on his rather ill-timed jest I went on to the house. I rang the bell, as Japp had closed the door behind him. After some moments it was opened to me by a middle-aged woman in black.

"Mr Havering will be here in a moment," I explained. "He has been detained by the inspector. I have come down with him from London to look into the case. Perhaps you can tell me briefly what occurred last night."

"Come inside, sir." She closed the door behind me, and we stood in the dimly-lighted hall. "It was after dinner last night, sir, that the man came. He asked to see Mr Pace, sir, and, seeing that he spoke the same way, I thought it was an American gentleman friend of Mr Pace's and I showed him into the gun room, and then went to tell Mr Pace. He wouldn't give any name, which, of course, was a bit odd, now I come to think of it. I told Mr Pace, and he seemed puzzled like, but he said to the mistress: 'Excuse me, Zoe, while I see what this fellow wants.' He went off to the gun room, and I went back to the kitchen, but after a while I heard loud voices, as if they were quarrelling, and I came out into the hall. At the same time, the mistress she comes out too, and just then there was a shot and then a dreadful silence. We both ran to the gun room door, but it was locked and we had to go round to the window. It was open, and there inside was Mr Pace, all shot and bleeding."

"What became of the man?"

"He must have got away through the window, sir, before we got to it."

"And then?"

"Mrs Havering sent me to fetch the police. Five miles to walk it was. They came back with me, and the constable he stayed all night, and this morning the police gentleman from London arrived."

"What was this man like who called to see Mr Pace?"

The housekeeper reflected.

"He had a black beard, sir, and was about middle-aged, and had on a light overcoat. Beyond the fact that he spoke like an American I didn't notice much about him."

"I see. Now I wonder if I can see Mrs Havering?"

"She's upstairs, sir. Shall I tell her?"

"If you please. Tell her that Mr Havering is outside with Inspector Japp, and that the gentleman he has brought back with him from London is anxious to speak to her as soon as possible."

"Very good, sir."

I was in a fever of impatience to get all the facts. Japp had two or three hours' start on me, and his anxiety to be gone made me keen to be close at his heels.

Mrs Havering did not keep me waiting long. In a few minutes I heard a light step descending the stairs, and looked up to see a very handsome young woman coming towards me. She wore a flame-coloured jumper that set off the slender boyishness of her figure. On her dark head was a little hat of flame-coloured leather. Even the present tragedy could not dim the vitality of her personality.

I introduced myself, and she nodded in quick comprehension.

"Of course I have often heard of you and your colleague, Monsieur Poirot. You have done some wonderful things together, haven't you? It was very clever of my husband to get you so promptly. Now will you ask me questions? That is the easiest way, isn't it, of getting to know all you want to about this dreadful affair?"

"Thank you, Mrs Havering. Now what time was it that this man arrived?"

"It must have been just before nine o'clock. We had finished dinner, and were sitting over our coffee and cigarettes."

"Your husband had already left for London?"

"Yes, he went up by the 6.15."

"Did he go by car to the station, or did he walk?"

"Our own car isn't down here. One came out from the garage in Elmer's Dale to fetch him in time for the train."

"Was Mr Pace quite his usual self?"

"Absolutely. Most normal in every way."

"Now, can you describe this visitor at all?"

"I'm afraid not. I didn't see him. Mrs Middleton showed him straight into the gun room and then came to tell my uncle."

"What did your uncle say?"

"He seemed rather annoyed, but went off at once. It was about five minutes later that I heard the sound of raised voices. I ran out into the hall and almost collided with Mrs Middleton. Then we heard the shot. The gun room door was locked on the inside, and we had to go right round the house to the window. Of course that took some time, and the murderer had been able to get well away. My poor uncle" — her voice faltered — "had been shot through the head. I saw at once that he was dead. I sent Mrs Middleton for the police. I was careful to touch nothing in the room but to leave it exactly as I found it."

I nodded approval.

"Now, as to the weapon?"

"Well, I can make a guess at it, Captain Hastings. A pair of revolvers of my husband's were mounted upon the wall. One of them is missing. I pointed this out to the police, and they took the other one away with them. When they have extracted the bullet, I suppose they will know for certain."

"May I go to the gun room?"

"Certainly. The police have finished with it. But the body has been removed."

She accompanied me to the scene of the crime. At that moment Havering entered the hall, and with a quick apology his wife ran to him. I was left to undertake my investigations alone.

I may as well confess at once that they were rather disappointing. In detective novels clues abound, but here I could find nothing that struck me as out of the ordinary except a large bloodstain on the carpet where I judged the dead man had fallen. I examined everything with painstaking care and took a couple of pictures of the room with my little camera which I had brought with me. I also examined the ground outside the window, but it appeared to have been so heavily trampled underfoot that I judged it was useless to waste time over it. No, I had seen all that Hunter's Lodge had to show me. I must go back to Elmer's Dale and get into touch with Japp. Accordingly I took leave of the Haverings, and was driven off in the car that had brought us up from the station.

I found Japp at the Matlock Arms and he took me forthwith to see the body. Harrington Pace was a small, spare, clean-shaven man, typically American in appearance. He had been shot through the back of the head, and the revolver had been discharged at close quarters.

"Turned away for a moment," remarked Japp, "and the other fellow snatched up a revolver and shot him. The one Mrs Havering handed over to us was fully loaded and I suppose the other one was also. Curious what darn fool things people do. Fancy keeping two loaded revolvers hanging up on your wall."

"What do you think of the case?" I asked, as we left the gruesome chamber behind us.

"Well, I'd got my eye on Havering to begin with. Oh, yes!" — noting my exclamation of astonishment. "Havering has one or two shady incidents in his past. When he was a boy at Oxford there was some funny business about the signature on one of his father's cheques. All hushed up of course. Then, he's pretty heavily in debt now, and they're the kind of debts he wouldn't like to go to his uncle about, whereas you may be sure the uncle's will would be in his favour. Yes, I'd got my eye on him, and that's why I wanted to speak to him before he saw his wife, but their statements dovetail all right, and I've been to the station and there's no doubt whatever that he left by the 6.15. That gets up to London about 10.30. He went straight to his club, he says, and if that's confirmed all right — why, he couldn't have been shooting his uncle here at nine o'clock in a black beard!"

"Ah, yes, I was going to ask you what you thought about that beard?"
Japp winked.

"I think it grew pretty fast — grew in the five miles from Elmer's Dale to Hunter's Lodge. Americans that I've met are mostly clean-shaven. Yes, it's amongst Mr Pace's American associates that we'll have to look for the murderer. I questioned the housekeeper first, and then her mistress, and their stories agree all right, but I'm sorry Mrs Havering didn't get a look at the fellow. She's a smart woman, and she might have noticed something that would set us on the track."

I sat down and wrote a minute and lengthy account to Poirot. I was able to add various further items of information before I posted the letter.

The bullet had been extracted and was proved to have been fired from a revolver identical with the one held by the police. Furthermore, Mr Havering's movements on the night in question had been checked and verified, and it was proved beyond doubt that he had actually arrived in London by the train in question. And, thirdly, a sensational development had occurred. A city gentleman, living at Ealing, on crossing Haven Green to get to the District Railway Station that morning, had observed a brown-paper parcel stuck between the railings. Opening it, he found that it contained a revolver. He handed the parcel over to the local police station, and before night it was proved to be the one we were in search of, the fellow to that given us by Mrs Havering. One bullet had been fired from it.

All this I added to my report. A wire from Poirot arrived whilst I was at breakfast the following morning:

OF COURSE BLACK-BEARDED MAN WAS NOT HAVERING ONLY YOU OR JAPP WOULD HAVE SUCH AN IDEA WIRE ME DESCRIPTION OF HOUSEKEEPER AND WHAT CLOTHES SHE WORE THIS MORNING SAME OF MRS HAVERING DO NOT WASTE TIME TAKING PHOTOGRAPHS OF INTERIORS THEY ARE UNDEREXPOSED AND NOT IN THE LEAST ARTISTIC.

It seemed to me that Poirot's style was unnecessarily facetious. I also fancied he was a shade jealous of my position on the spot with full facilities for handling the case. His request for a description of the clothes worn by the two women appeared to me to be simply ridiculous, but I complied as well as I, a mere man, was able to.

At eleven a reply wire came from Poirot:

ADVISE JAPP ARREST HOUSEKEEPER BEFORE IT IS TOO LATE.

Dumbfounded, I took the wire to Japp. He swore softly under his breath.

"He's the goods, Monsieur Poirot! If he says so, there's something in it. And I hardly noticed the woman. I don't know that I can go so far as arresting her, but I'll have her watched. We'll go up right away, and take another look at her."

But it was too late. Mrs Middleton, that quiet middle-aged woman, who had appeared so normal and respectable, had vanished into thin air. Her box had been left behind. It contained only ordinary wearing apparel. There was no clue in it to her identity, or as to her whereabouts.

From Mrs Havering we elicited all the facts we could:

"I engaged her about three weeks ago when Mrs Emery, our former housekeeper, left. She came to me from Mrs Selbourne's Agency in Mount Street — a very well-known place. I get all my servants from there. They sent several women to see me, but this Mrs Middleton seemed much the nicest, and had splendid references. I engaged her on the spot, and notified the Agency of the fact. I can't believe that there was anything wrong with her. She was such a nice quiet woman."

The thing was certainly a mystery. Whilst it was clear that the woman herself could not have committed the crime, since at the moment the shot was fired Mrs Havering was with her in the hall, nevertheless she must have some connection with the murder, or why should she suddenly take to her heels and bolt?

I wired the latest development to Poirot and suggested returning to London and making inquiries at Selbourne's Agency.

Poirot's reply was prompt:

USELESS TO INQUIRE AT AGENCY THEY WILL NEVER HAVE HEARD OF HER FIND OUT WHAT VEHICLE TOOK HER UP TO HUNTER'S LODGE WHEN SHE FIRST ARRIVED THERE.

Though mystified, I was obedient. The means of transport in Elmer's Dale were limited. The local garage had two battered Ford cars, and there were two station flies. None of these had been requisitioned on the date in question. Questioned, Mrs Havering explained that she had given the woman the money for her fare down to Derbyshire and sufficient to hire a car or fly to take her up to Hunter's Lodge. There was usually one of the Fords at the station on the chance of its being required. Taking into consideration the further fact that nobody at the station had noticed the arrival of a stranger, black-bearded or otherwise, on the fatal evening, everything seemed to point to the conclusion that the murderer had come to the spot in a car, which had been waiting near at hand to aid his escape, and that the same car had brought the mysterious housekeeper to her new post. I may mention that inquiries at the Agency in London bore out Poirot's prognostication. No such woman as "Mrs Middleton" had ever been on their books. They had received the Hon.* Mrs Havering's application for a housekeeper, and had sent her various applicants for the post. When she sent them the engagement fee, she omitted to mention which woman she had selected.

Somewhat crestfallen, I returned to London. I found Poirot established in an armchair by the fire in a garish, silk dressing gown. He

---

*Hon.: short for *Honourable*, a title used by British people whose parents or whose husband's or wife's parents have a very high social rank.

greeted me with much affection.

"*Mon ami* Hastings! But how glad I am to see you. Veritably I have for you a great affection! And you have enjoyed yourself? You have run to and fro with the good Japp? You have interrogated and investigated to your heart's content?"

"Poirot," I cried, "the thing's a dark mystery! It will never be solved."

"It is true that we are not likely to cover ourselves with glory over it."

"No, indeed. It's a hard nut to crack."

"Oh, as far as that goes, I am very good at cracking the nuts! A veritable squirrel! It is not that which embarrasses me. I know well enough who killed Mr Harrington Pace."

"You know? How did you find out?"

"Your illuminating answers to my wires supplied me with the truth. See here, Hastings, let us examine the facts methodically and in order. Mr Harrington Pace is a man with a considerable fortune which at his death will doubtless pass to his nephew. Point No. 1. His nephew is known to be desperately hard up. Point No. 2. His nephew is also known to be — shall we say a man of rather loose moral fibre. Point No. 3."

"But Roger Havering is proved to have journeyed straight up to London."

"*Précisément* — and therefore, as Mr Havering left Elmer's Dale at 6.15, and since Mr Pace cannot have been killed before he left, or the doctor would have spotted the time of the crime as being given wrongly when he examined the body, we conclude quite rightly, that Mr Havering did *not* shoot his uncle. But there is a Mrs Havering, Hastings."

"Impossible! The housekeeper was with her when the shot was fired."

"Ah, yes, the housekeeper. But she has disappeared."

"She will be found."

"I think not. There is something peculiarly elusive about that housekeeper, don't you think so, Hastings? It struck me at once."

"She played her part, I suppose, and then got out in the nick of time."

"And what was her part?"

"Well, presumably to admit her confederate, the black-bearded man."

"Oh, no, that was not her part! Her part was what you have just mentioned, to provide an alibi for Mrs Havering at the moment the shot was fired. And no one will ever find her, *mon ami*, because she does not exist! 'There's no such person', as your so great Shakespeare says."

"It was Dickens," I murmured, unable to suppress a smile. "But what do you mean, Poirot?"

"I mean that Zoe Havering was an actress before her marriage, that you and Japp only saw the housekeeper in a dark hall, a dim middle-aged figure in black with a faint subdued voice, and finally that neither you nor Japp, nor the local police whom the housekeeper fetched, ever saw Mrs Middleton and her mistress at one and the same time. It was child's play for that clever and daring woman. On the pretext of summoning her mistress, she runs upstairs, slips on a bright jumper and a hat with black curls attached which she jams down over the grey transformation. A few deft touches, and the make-up is removed, a slight dusting of rouge, and the brilliant Zoe Havering comes down with her clear ringing voice. Nobody looks particularly at the housekeeper. Why should they? There is nothing to connect her with the crime. She, too, has an alibi."

"But the revolver that was found at Ealing? Mrs Havering could not have placed it there?"

"No, that was Roger Havering's job — but it was a mistake on their part. It put me on the right track. A man who has committed murder with a revolver which he found on the spot would fling it away at once, he would not carry it up to London with him. No, the motive was clear, the criminals wished to focus the interest of the police on a spot far removed from Derbyshire, they were anxious to get the police away as soon as possible from the vicinity of Hunter's Lodge. Of course the revolver found at Ealing was not the one with which Mr Pace was shot.

Roger Havering discharged one shot from it, brought it up to London, went straight to his club to establish his alibi, then went quickly out to Ealing by the District, a matter of about twenty minutes only, placed the parcel where it was found and so back to town. That charming creature, his wife, quietly shoots Mr Pace after dinner — you remember he was shot from behind? Another significant point, that! — reloads the revolver and puts it back in its place, and then starts off with her desperate little comedy."

"It's incredible," I murmured, fascinated, "and yet——"

"And yet it is true. *Bien sûr*, my friend, it is true. But to bring that precious pair to justice, that is another matter. Well, Japp must do what he can — I have written him fully — but I very much fear, Hastings, that we shall be obliged to leave them to Fate, or *le bon Dieu*, whichever you prefer."

"The wicked flourish like a green bay tree," I reminded him.

"But at a price, Hastings, always at a price, *croyez-moi*!"

Poirot's forebodings were confirmed. Japp, though convinced of the truth of his theory, was unable to get together the necessary evidence to ensure a conviction.

Mr Pace's huge fortune passed into the hands of his murderers. Nevertheless, Nemesis did overtake them, and when I read in the paper that the Hon. Roger and Mrs Havering were amongst those killed in the crashing of the Air Mail to Paris I knew that Justice was satisfied.

The Million Dollar Bond Robbery

"What a number of bond robberies there have been lately!" I observed one morning, laying aside the newspaper. "Poirot, let us forsake the science of detection, and take to crime instead!"

"You are on the — how do you say it? — get-rich-quick tack, eh, *mon ami?*"

"Well, look at this last *coup*, the million dollars' worth of Liberty Bonds which the London and Scottish Bank were sending to New York, and which disappeared in such a remarkable manner on board the *Olympia*."

"If it were not for the *mal de mer*, and the difficulty of practising the so excellent method of Laverguier for a longer time than the few hours of crossing the Channel, I should delight to voyage myself on one of these big liners," murmured Poirot dreamily.

"Yes, indeed," I said enthusiastically. "Some of them must be perfect palaces; the swimming baths, the lounges, the restaurant, the palm courts — really, it must be hard to believe that one is on the sea."

"Me, I always know when I am on the sea," said Poirot sadly. "And all those bagatelles that you enumerate, they say nothing to me; but, my friend, consider for a moment the geniuses that travel as it were incognito! On board these floating palaces, as you so justly call them, one would meet the elite, the *haute noblesse* of the criminal world!"

I laughed.

"So that's the way your enthusiasm runs! You would have liked to cross swords with the man who sneaked the Liberty Bonds?"

The landlady interrupted us.

"A young lady as wants to see you, Mr Poirot. Here's her card."

The card bore the inscription: Miss Esmée Farquhar, and Poirot, after diving under the table to retrieve a stray crumb, and putting it carefully in the wastepaper basket, nodded to the landlady to admit her.

In another minute one of the most charming girls I have ever seen was ushered into the room. She was perhaps about five-and-twenty, with big brown eyes and a perfect figure. She was well-dressed and perfectly composed in manner.

"Sit down, I beg of you, Mademoiselle. This is my friend, Captain Hastings, who aids me in my little problems."

"I am afraid it is a big problem I have brought you today, Monsieur Poirot," said the girl, giving me a pleasant bow as she seated herself. "I daresay you have read about it in the papers. I am referring to the theft of Liberty Bonds on the *Olympia*." Some astonishment must have shown itself on Poirot's face, for she continued quickly: "You are doubtless asking yourself what I have to do with a grave institution like the London and Scottish Bank. In one sense nothing, in another sense everything. You see, Monsieur Poirot, I am engaged to Mr Philip Ridgeway."

"Aha! and Mr Philip Ridgeway——"

"Was in charge of the bonds when they were stolen. Of course no actual blame can attach to him, it was not his fault in any way. Nevertheless, he is half distraught over the matter, and his uncle, I know, insists that he must carelessly have mentioned having them in his possession. It is a terrible setback to his career."

"Who is his uncle?"

"Mr Vavasour, joint general manager of the London and Scottish Bank."

"Suppose, Miss Farquhar, that you recount to me the whole story?"

"Very well. As you know, the Bank wished to extend their credits in America, and for this purpose decided to send over a million dollars in Liberty Bonds. Mr Vavasour selected his nephew, who had occupied a position of trust in the Bank for many years and who was conversant with all the details of the Bank's dealings in New York, to make the trip. The

Olympia sailed from Liverpool on the 23rd, and the bonds were handed over to Philip on the morning of that day by Mr Vavasour and Mr Shaw, the two joint general managers of the London and Scottish Bank. They were counted, enclosed in a package, and sealed in his presence, and he then locked the package at once in his portmanteau."

"A portmanteau with an ordinary lock?"

"No, Mr Shaw insisted on a special lock being fitted to it by Hubbs's. Philip, as I say, placed the package at the bottom of the trunk. It was stolen just a few hours before reaching New York. A rigorous search of the whole ship was made, but without result. The bonds seemed literally to have vanished into thin air."

Poirot made a grimace.

"But they did not vanish absolutely, since I gather that they were sold in small parcels within half an hour of the docking of the *Olympia*! Well, undoubtedly the next thing is for me to see Mr Ridgeway."

"I was about to suggest that you should lunch with me at the 'Cheshire Cheese'. Philip will be there. He is meeting me, but does not yet know that I have been consulting you on his behalf."

We agreed to this suggestion readily enough, and drove there in a taxi.

Mr Philip Ridgeway was there before us, and looked somewhat surprised to see his fiancée arriving with two complete strangers. He was a nice-looking young fellow, tall and spruce, with a touch of greying hair at the temples, though he could not have been much over thirty.

Miss Farquhar went up to him and laid her hand on his arm.

"You must forgive me acting without consulting you, Philip," she said. "Let me introduce you to Monsieur Hercule Poirot, of whom you must often have heard, and his friend, Captain Hastings."

Ridgeway looked very astonished.

"Of course I have heard of you, Monsieur Poirot," he said, as he shook hands. "But I had no idea that Esmée was thinking of consulting you about my — our trouble."

"I was afraid you would not let me do it, Philip," said Miss Farquhar meekly.

"So you took care to be on the safe side," he observed, with a smile. "I hope Monsieur Poirot will be able to throw some light on this extraordinary puzzle, for I confess frankly that I am nearly out of my mind with worry and anxiety about it."

Indeed, his face looked drawn and haggard and showed only too clearly the strain under which he was labouring.

"Well, well," said Poirot. "Let us lunch, and over lunch we will put our heads together and see what can be done. I want to hear Mr Ridgeway's story from his own lips."

Whilst we devoured the excellent steak and kidney pudding of the establishment, Philip Ridgeway narrated the circumstances leading to the disappearance of the bonds. His story agreed with that of Miss Farquhar in every particular. When he had finished, Poirot took up the thread with a question.

"What exactly led you to discover that the bonds had been stolen, Mr Ridgeway?"

He laughed rather bitterly.

"The thing stared me in the face, Monsieur Poirot. I couldn't have missed it. My cabin trunk was half out from under the bunk and all scratched and cut about where they'd tried to force the lock."

"But I understood that it had been opened with a key?"

"That's so. They tried to force it, but couldn't. And, in the end, they must have got it unlocked somehow or other."

"Curious," said Poirot, his eyes beginning to flicker with the green light I knew so well. "Very curious! They waste much, much time trying to prise it open, and then — *sapristi*! they find that they have the key all the time — for each of Hubbs's locks are unique."

"That's just why they couldn't have had the key. It never left me day or night."

"You are sure of that?"

"I can swear to it, and besides, if they had had the key or a duplicate, why should they waste time trying to force an obviously unforceable lock?"

"Ah! there is exactly the question we are asking ourselves! I venture to prophesy that the solution, if we ever find it, will hinge on that curious fact. I beg of you not to assault me if I ask you one more question: *Are you perfectly certain that you did not leave the trunk unlocked?*"

Philip Ridgeway merely looked at him, and Poirot gesticulated apologetically.

"Ah, but these things can happen, I assure you! Very well, the bonds were stolen from the trunk. What did the thief do with them? How did he manage to get ashore with them?"

"Ah!" cried Ridgeway. "That's just it. How? Word was passed to the Customs authorities, and every soul that left the ship was gone over with a toothcomb!"

"And the bonds, I gather, made a bulky package?"

"Certainly they did. They could hardly have been hidden on board — and anyway we know they weren't, because they were offered for sale within half an hour of the *Olympia*'s arrival, long before I got the cables going and the numbers sent out. One broker swears he bought some of them even before the *Olympia* got in. But you can't send bonds by wireless."

"Not by wireless, but did any tug come alongside?"

"Only the official ones, and that was after the alarm was given when everyone was on the lookout. I was watching out myself for their being passed over to someone that way. My God, Monsieur Poirot, this thing will drive me mad! People are beginning to say I stole them myself."

"But you also were searched on landing, weren't you?" asked Poirot gently.

"Yes."

The young man stared at him in a puzzled manner.

"You do not catch my meaning, I see," said Poirot, smiling enigmatically. "Now I should like to make a few inquiries at the Bank."

Ridgeway produced a card and scribbled a few words on it.

"Send this in and my uncle will see you at once."

Poirot thanked him, bade farewell to Miss Farquhar, and together we started out for Threadneedle Street and the head office of the London and Scottish Bank. On production of Ridgeway's card, we were led through the labyrinth of counters and desks, skirting paying-in clerks and paying-out clerks and up to a small office on the first floor where the joint general managers received us. They were two grave gentlemen, who had grown grey in the service of the Bank. Mr Vavasour had a short white beard, Mr Shaw was clean-shaven.

"I understand you are strictly a private inquiry agent?" said Mr Vavasour. "Quite so, quite so. We have, of course, placed ourselves in the hands of Scotland Yard. Inspector McNeil has charge of the case. A very able officer, I believe."

"I am sure of it," said Poirot politely. "You will permit a few questions, on your nephew's behalf? About this lock, who ordered it from Hubbs's?"

"I ordered it myself," said Mr Shaw. "I would not trust to any clerk in the matter. As to the keys, Mr Ridgeway had one, and the other two are held by my colleague and myself."

"And no clerk has had access to them?"

Mr Shaw turned inquiringly to Mr Vavasour.

"I think I am correct in saying that they have remained in the safe where we placed them on the 23rd," said Mr Vavasour. "My colleague was unfortunately taken ill a fortnight ago — in fact on the very day that Philip left us. He has only just recovered."

"Severe bronchitis is no joke to a man of my age," said Mr Shaw ruefully. "But I'm afraid Mr Vavasour has suffered from the hard work entailed by my absence, especially with this unexpected worry coming on top of everything."

Poirot asked a few more questions. I judged that he was endeavouring to gauge the exact amount of intimacy between uncle and nephew. Mr Vavasour's answers were brief and punctilious. His nephew was a trusted official of the Bank, and had no debts or money difficulties that he knew of. He had been entrusted with similar missions in the past. Finally we were politely bowed out.

"I am disappointed," said Poirot, as we emerged into the street.

"You hoped to discover more? They are such stodgy old men."

"It is not their stodginess which disappoints me, *mon ami*. I do not expect to find in a Bank manager a 'keen financier with an eagle glance', as your favourite works of fiction put it. No, I am disappointed in the case — it is too easy!"

"*Easy?*"

"Yes, do you not find it almost childishly simple?"

"You know who stole the bonds?"

"I do."

"But then — we must — why——"

"Do not confuse and fluster yourself, Hastings. We are not going to do anything at present."

"But why? What are you waiting for?"

"For the *Olympia*. She is due on her return trip from New York on Tuesday."

"But if you know who stole the bonds, why wait? He may escape."

"To a South Sea island where there is no extradition? No, *mon ami*, he would find life very uncongenial there. As to why I wait — *eh bien*, to the intelligence of Hercule Poirot the case is perfectly clear, but for the benefit of others, not so greatly gifted by the good God — the Inspector McNeil, for instance — it would be as well to make a few inquiries to establish the facts. One must have consideration for those less gifted than oneself."

"Good Lord, Poirot! Do you know, I'd give a considerable sum of money to see you make a thorough ass of yourself — just for once. You're so confoundedly conceited!"

"Do not enrage yourself, Hastings. In verity, I observe that there are times when you almost detest me! Alas, I suffer the penalties of greatness!"

The little man puffed out his chest, and sighed so comically that I was forced to laugh.

Tuesday saw us speeding to Liverpool in a first-class carriage of the L & NWR.* Poirot had obstinately refused to enlighten me as to his suspicions — or certainties. He contented himself with expressing surprise that I, too, was not equally *au fait* with the situation. I disdained to argue, and entrenched my curiosity behind a rampart of pretended indifference.

Once arrived at the quay alongside which lay the big transatlantic liner, Poirot became brisk and alert. Our proceedings consisted in interviewing four successive stewards and inquiring after a friend of Poirot's who had crossed to New York on the 23rd.

"An elderly gentleman, wearing glasses. A great invalid, hardly moved out of his cabin."

The description appeared to tally with one Mr Ventnor who had occupied the cabin C24 which was next to that of Philip Ridgeway. Although unable to see how Poirot had deduced Mr Ventnor's existence and personal appearance, I was keenly excited.

"Tell me," I cried, "was this gentleman one of the first to land when you got to New York?"

The steward shook his head.

"No, indeed, sir, he was one of the last off the boat."

I retired crestfallen, and observed Poirot grinning at me. He thanked

*L & NWR: the London and North Western Railway Company

the steward, a note changed hands, and we took our departure.

"It's all very well," I remarked heatedly, "but that last answer must have damned your precious theory, grin as you please!"

"As usual, you see nothing, Hastings. That last answer is, on the contrary, the copingstone of my theory."

I flung up my hands in despair.

"I give it up."

When we were in the train, speeding towards London, Poirot wrote busily for a few minutes, sealing up the result in an envelope.

"This is for the good Inspector McNeil. We will leave it at Scotland Yard in passing, and then to the Rendezvous Restaurant, where I have asked Miss Esmée Farquhar to do us the honour of dining with us."

"What about Ridgeway?"

"What about him?" asked Poirot with a twinkle.

"Why, you surely don't think — you can't——"

"The habit of incoherence is growing upon you, Hastings. As a matter of fact I *did* think. If Ridgeway had been the thief — which was perfectly possible — the case would have been charming; a piece of neat methodical work."

"But not so charming for Miss Farquhar."

"Possibly you are right. Therefore all is for the best. Now, Hastings, let us review the case. I can see that you are dying to do so. The sealed package is removed from the trunk and vanishes, as Miss Farquhar puts it, into thin air. We will dismiss the thin air theory, which is not practicable at the present stage of science, and consider what is likely to have become of it. Everyone asserts the incredulity of its being smuggled ashore——"

"Yes, but we know——"

"*You* may know, Hastings, I do not. I take the view that, since it seemed incredible, it *was* incredible. Two possibilities remain: it was hidden on board — also rather difficult — or it was thrown overboard."

"With a cork on it, do you mean?"

"Without a cork."

I stared.

"But if the bonds were thrown overboard, they couldn't have been sold in New York."

"I admire your logical mind, Hastings. The bonds were sold in New York, therefore they were not thrown overboard. You see where that leads us?"

"Where we were when we started."

"*Jamais de la vie!* If the package was thrown overboard and the bonds were sold in New York, the package could not have contained the bonds. Is there any evidence that the package *did* contain the bonds? Remember, Mr Ridgeway never opened it from the time it was placed in his hands in London."

"Yes, but then——"

Poirot waved an impatient hand.

"Permit me to continue. The last moment that the bonds are seen as bonds is in the office of the London and Scottish Bank on the morning of the 23rd. They reappear in New York half an hour after the *Olympia* gets in, and according to one man, whom nobody listens to, actually *before* she gets in. Supposing then, that they have never been on the *Olympia* at all? Is there any other way they could get to New York? Yes. The *Gigantic* leaves Southampton on the same day as the *Olympia*, and she holds the record for the Atlantic. Mailed by the *Gigantic*, the bonds would be in New York the day before the *Olympia* arrived. All is clear, the case begins to explain itself. The sealed packet is only a dummy, and the moment of its substitution must be in the office in the Bank. It would be an easy matter for any of the three men present to have prepared a duplicate package which could be substituted for the genuine one. *Très bien*, the bonds are mailed to a confederate in New York, with instructions to sell as soon as the *Olympia* is in, but someone must travel on the *Olympia* to engineer the supposed moment of the robbery."

"But why?"

"Because if Ridgeway merely opens the packet and finds it a dummy, suspicion flies at once to London. No, the man on board in the cabin next door does his work, pretends to force the lock in an obvious manner so as to draw immediate attention to the theft, really unlocks the trunk with a duplicate key, throws the package overboard and waits until the last to leave the boat. Naturally he wears glasses to conceal his eyes, and is an invalid since he does not want to run the risk of meeting Ridgeway. He steps ashore in New York and returns by the first boat available."

"But who — which was he?"

"The man who had a duplicate key, the man who ordered the lock, the man who has *not* been severely ill with bronchitis at his home in the country — *enfin*, the 'stodgy' old man, Mr Shaw! There are criminals in high places sometimes, my friend. Ah, here we are. Mademoiselle, I have succeeded! You permit?"

And, beaming, Poirot kissed the astonished girl lightly on either cheek!

The Adventure of the Clapham Cook

At the time that I was sharing rooms with my friend Hercule Poirot, it was my custom to read aloud to him the headlines in the morning newspaper, *The Daily Blare*.

The Daily Blare was a paper that made the most of any opportunity for sensationalism. Robberies and murders did not lurk obscurely in its back pages. Instead they hit you in the eye in large type on the front page.

"'Absconding Bank Clerk Disappears with Fifty Thousand Pounds' Worth of Negotiable Securities,'" I read. "'Husband Puts his Head in Gas Oven. Unhappy Home Life. Missing Typist. Pretty Girl of Twenty-One: Where is Edna Field?'"

"There you are, Poirot, plenty to choose from. An absconding bank clerk, a mysterious suicide, a missing typist — which will you have?"

My friend was in a placid mood. He quietly shook his head.

"I am not greatly attracted to any of them, *mon ami*. Today I feel inclined for the life of ease. It would have to be a very interesting problem to tempt me from my chair. See you, I have affairs of importance of my own to attend to."

"Such as?"

"My wardrobe, Hastings. If I mistake not, there is on my new grey suit the spot of grease — only the unique spot, but it is sufficient to trouble me. Then there is my winter overcoat — I must lay him aside in the powder of Keatings. And I think — yes, I think — the moment is ripe for the trimming of my moustaches — and afterwards I must apply the *pommade*."

"Well," I said, strolling to the window, "I doubt if you'll be able to carry out this delirious programme. That was a ring at the bell. You have a client."

"Unless the affair is one of national importance, I touch it not," declared Poirot with dignity.

A moment later our privacy was invaded by a stout red-faced lady who panted audibly as a result of her rapid ascent of the stairs.

"You're M. Poirot?" she demanded, as she sank into a chair.

"I am Hercule Poirot, yes, Madame."

"You're not a bit like what I thought you'd be," said the lady, eyeing him with some disfavour. "Did you pay for the bit in the paper saying what a clever detective you were, or did they put it in themselves?"

"Madame!" said Poirot, drawing himself up.

"I'm sorry, I'm sure, but you know what these papers are nowadays. You begin reading a nice article 'What a bride said to her plain unmarried friend', and it's all about a simple thing you buy at the chemist's and shampoo your hair with. Nothing but puff. But no offence taken, I hope? I'll tell you what I want you to do for me. I want you to find my cook."

Poirot stared at her; for once his ready tongue failed him. I turned aside to hide the broadening smile I could not control.

"It's all this wicked dole," continued the lady. "Putting ideas into servants' heads, wanting to be typists and what nots. Stop the dole, that's what I say. I'd like to know what *my* servants have to complain of — afternoon and evening off a week, alternate Sundays, washing put out, same food as we have — and never a bit of margarine in the house, nothing but the very best butter."

She paused for want of breath and Poirot seized his opportunity. He spoke in his haughtiest manner, rising to his feet as he did so.

"I fear you are making a mistake, Madame. I am not holding an inquiry into the conditions of domestic service. I am a private detective."

"I know that," said our visitor. "Didn't I tell you I wanted you to find my cook for me? Walked out of the house on Wednesday, without so much as a word to me, and never came back."

"I am sorry, Madame, but I do not touch this particular kind of business. I wish you good morning."

Our visitor snorted with indignation.

"That's it, is it, my fine fellow? Too proud, eh? Only deal with Government secrets and Countesses' jewels? Let me tell you a servant's every bit as important as a tiara to a woman in my position. We can't all be fine ladies going out in our motors with our diamonds and our pearls. A good cook's a good cook — and when you lose her, it's as much to you as her pearls are to some fine lady."

For a moment or two it appeared to be a toss up between Poirot's dignity and his sense of humour. Finally he laughed and sat down again.

"Madame, you are in the right, and I am in the wrong. Your remarks are just and intelligent. This case will be a novelty. Never yet have I hunted a missing domestic. Truly here is the problem of national importance that I was demanding of fate just before your arrival. *En avant!* You say this jewel of a cook went out on Wednesday and did not return. That is the day before yesterday."

"Yes, it was her day out."

"But probably, Madame, she has met with some accident. Have you inquired at any of the hospitals?"

"That's exactly what I thought yesterday, but this morning, if you please, she sent for her box. And not so much as a line to me! If I'd been at home, I'd not have let it go — treating me like that! But I'd just stepped out to the butcher."

"Will you describe her to me?"

"She was middle-aged, stout, black hair turning grey — most respectable. She'd been ten years in her last place. Eliza Dunn, her name was."

"And you had had — no disagreement with her on the Wednesday?"

"None whatsoever. That's what makes it all so queer."

"How many servants do you keep, Madame?"

"Two. The house-parlourmaid, Annie, is a very nice girl. A bit forgetful and her head full of young men, but a good servant if you keep her up to her work."

"Did she and the cook get on well together?"

"They had their ups and downs, of course — but on the whole, very well."

"And the girl can throw no light on the mystery?"

"She says not — but you know what servants are — they all hang together."

"Well, well, we must look into this. Where did you say you resided, Madame?"

"At Clapham; 88 Prince Albert Road."

"*Bien*, Madame, I will wish you good morning, and you may count upon seeing me at your residence during the course of the day."

Mrs Todd, for such was our new friend's name, then took her departure. Poirot looked at me somewhat ruefully.

"Well, well, Hastings, this is a novel affair that we have here. The Disappearance of the Clapham Cook! Never, *never*, must our friend Inspector Japp get to hear of this!"

He then proceeded to heat an iron and carefully removed the grease spot from his grey suit by means of a piece of blotting paper. His moustaches he regretfully postponed to another day, and we set out for Clapham.

Prince Albert Road proved to be a street of small prim houses, all exactly alike, with neat lace curtains veiling the windows, and well-polished brass knockers on the doors.

We rang the bell at No. 88, and the door was opened by a neat maid with a pretty face. Mrs Todd came out in the hall to greet us.

"Don't go, Annie," she cried. "This gentleman's a detective and he'll want to ask you some questions."

Annie's face displayed a struggle between alarm and a pleasurable excitement.

"I thank you, Madame," said Poirot bowing. "I would like to question your maid now — and to see her alone, if I may."

We were shown into a small drawing room, and when Mrs Todd, with obvious reluctance, had left the room, Poirot commenced his cross-examination.

"*Voyons*, Mademoiselle Annie, all that you shall tell us will be of the greatest importance. You alone can shed any light on the case. Without your assistance I can do nothing."

The alarm vanished from the girl's face and the pleasurable excitement became more strongly marked.

"I'm sure, sir," she said, "I'll tell you anything I can."

"That is good," Poirot beamed approval on her. "Now, first of all what is your own idea? You are a girl of remarkable intelligence. That can be seen at once! What is your own explanation of Eliza's disappearance?"

Thus encouraged, Annie fairly flowed into excited speech.

"White Slavers,* sir, I've said so all along! Cook was always warning me against them. 'Don't you sniff no scent, or eat any sweets — no matter how gentlemanly the fellow!' Those were her words to me. And now they've got her! I'm sure of it. As likely as not, she's been shipped to Turkey or one of them Eastern places where I've heard they like them fat!"

Poirot preserved an admirable gravity.

"But in that case — and it is indeed an idea! — would she have sent for her trunk?"

"Well, I don't know, sir. She'd want her things — even in those foreign places."

"Who came for the trunk — a man?"

"It was Carter Paterson, sir."

"Did you pack it?"

---

*White Slavers: people who take girls to foreign countries and force them to live immorally

"No, sir, it was already packed and corded."

"Ah! that's interesting. That shows that when she left the house on Wednesday, she had already determined not to return. You see that, do you not?"

"Yes, sir." Annie looked slightly taken aback. "I hadn't thought of that. But it might still have been White Slavers, mightn't it, sir?" she added wistfully.

"Undoubtedly!" said Poirot gravely. He went on: "Did you both occupy the same bedroom?"

"No, sir, we had separate rooms."

"And had Eliza expressed any dissatisfaction with her present post to you at all? Were you both happy here?"

"She'd never mentioned leaving. The place is all right——" The girl hesitated.

"Speak freely," said Poirot kindly. "I shall not tell your mistress."

"Well, of course, sir, she's a caution, Missus is. But the food's good. Plenty of it, and no stinting. Something hot for supper, good outings, and as much frying-fat as you like. And anyway, if Eliza did want to make a change, she'd never have gone off this way, I'm sure. She'd have stayed her month. Why, Missus could have a month's wages out of her for doing this!"

"And the work, it is not too hard?"

"Well, she's particular — always poking round in corners and looking for dust. And then there's the lodger, or paying guest as he's always called. But that's only breakfast and dinner, same as Master. They're out all day in the City."*

"You like your master?"

"He's all right — very quiet and a bit on the stingy side."

"You can't remember, I suppose, the last thing Eliza said before she went out?"

*the City: an area of central London which is Britain's financial centre

"Yes, I can. 'If there's any stewed peaches over from the dining room,' she says, 'we'll have them for supper, and a bit of bacon and some fried potatoes.' Mad over stewed peaches, she was. I shouldn't wonder if they didn't get her that way."

"Was Wednesday her regular day out?"

"Yes, she had Wednesdays and I had Thursdays."

Poirot asked a few more questions, then declared himself satisfied. Annie departed, and Mrs Todd hurried in, her face alight with curiosity. She had, I felt certain, bitterly resented her exclusion from the room during our conversation with Annie. Poirot, however, was careful to soothe her feelings tactfully.

"It is difficult," he explained, "for a woman of exceptional intelligence such as yourself, Madame, to bear patiently the roundabout methods we poor detectives are forced to use. To have patience with stupidity is difficult for the quick-witted."

Having thus charmed away any little resentment on Mrs Todd's part, he brought the conversation round to her husband and elicited the information that he worked with a firm in the City and would not be home until after six.

"Doubtless he is very disturbed and worried by this unaccountable business, eh? Is it not so?"

"He's never worried," declared Mrs Todd. " 'Well, well, get another, my dear.' That's all *he* said! He's so calm that it drives me to distraction sometimes. 'An ungrateful woman,' he said. 'We are well rid of her.' "

"What about the other inmates of the house, Madame?"

"You mean Mr Simpson, our paying guest? Well, as long as he gets his breakfast and his evening meal all right, *he* doesn't worry."

"What is his profession, Madame?"

"He works in a bank." She mentioned its name, and I started slightly, remembering my perusal of *The Daily Blare*.

"A young man?"

"Twenty-eight, I believe. Nice quiet young fellow."

"I should like to have a few words with him, and also with your husband, if I may. I will return for that purpose this evening. I venture to suggest that you should repose yourself a little, Madame, you look fatigued."

"I should just think I am! First the worry about Eliza, and then I was at the Sales practically all yesterday, and you know what *that* is, M. Poirot, and what with one thing and another and a lot to do in the house, because of course Annie can't do it all — and very likely she'll give notice anyway, being unsettled in this way — well, what with it all, I'm tired out!"

Poirot murmured sympathetically, and we took our leave.

"It's a curious coincidence," I said, "but that absconding clerk, Davis, was from the same bank as Simpson. Can there be any connection, do you think?"

Poirot smiled.

"At the one end, a defaulting clerk, at the other a vanishing cook. It is hard to see any relation between the two, unless possibly Davis visited Simpson, fell in love with the cook, and persuaded her to accompany him on his flight!"

I laughed. But Poirot remained grave.

"He might have done worse," he said reprovingly. "Remember, Hastings, if you are going into exile, a good cook may be of more comfort than a pretty face!" He paused for a moment and then went on. "It is a curious case, full of contradictory features. I am interested — yes, I am distinctly interested."

That evening we returned to 88 Prince Albert Road and interviewed both Todd and Simpson. The former was a melancholy lantern-jawed man of forty-odd.

"Oh! yes, yes," he said vaguely. "Eliza. Yes. A good cook, I believe. And economical. I make a strong point of economy."

"Can you imagine any reason for her leaving you so suddenly?"

"Oh! well," said Mr Todd vaguely. "Servants, you know. My wife worries too much. Worn out from always worrying. The whole problem's quite simple really. 'Get another, my dear,' I say. 'Get another.' That's all there is to it. No good crying over spilt milk."

Mr Simpson was equally unhelpful. He was a quiet inconspicuous young man with spectacles.

"I must have seen her, I suppose," he said. "Elderly woman, wasn't she? Of course, it's the other one I see always, Annie. Nice girl. Very obliging."

"Were those two on good terms with each other?"

Mr Simpson said he couldn't say, he was sure. He supposed so.

"Well, we get nothing of interest there, *mon ami*," said Poirot as we left the house. Our departure had been delayed by a burst of vociferous repetition from Mrs Todd, who repeated everything she had said that morning at rather greater length.

"Are you disappointed?" I asked. "Did you expect to hear something?"

Poirot shook his head.

"There was a possibility, of course," he said. "But I hardly thought it likely."

The next development was a letter which Poirot received on the following morning. He read it, turned purple with indignation, and handed it to me.

Mrs Todd regrets that after all she will not avail herself of M. Poirot's services. After talking the matter over with her husband she sees that it is foolish to call in a detective about a purely domestic affair. Mrs Todd encloses a guinea for consultation fee.

"Aha!" cried Poirot angrily. "And they think to get rid of Hercule

Poirot like that! As a favour — a great favour — I consent to investigate their miserable little twopenny-halfpenny affair — and they dismiss me *comme ça*! Here, I mistake not, is the hand of Mr Todd. But I say no! — thirty-six times no! I will spend my own guineas, thirty-six hundred of them if need be, but I will get to the bottom of this matter!"

"Yes," I said. "But how?"

Poirot calmed down a little.

"*D'abord*," he said, "we will advertise in the papers. Let me see — yes — something like this: 'If Eliza Dunn will communicate with this address, she will hear of something to her advantage.' Put it in all the papers you can think of, Hastings. Then I will make some little inquiries of my own. Go, go — all must be done as quickly as possible!"

I did not see him again until the evening, when he condescended to tell me what he had been doing.

"I have made inquiries at the firm of Mr Todd. He was not absent on Wednesday, and he bears a good character — so much for him. Then Simpson, on Thursday he was ill and did not come to the bank, but he was there on Wednesday. He was moderately friendly with Davis. Nothing out of the common. There does not seem to be anything there. No. We must place our reliance on the advertisement."

The advertisement duly appeared in all the principal daily papers. By Poirot's orders it was to be continued every day for a week. His eagerness over this uninteresting matter of a defaulting cook was extraordinary, but I realised that he considered it a point of honour to persevere until he finally succeeded. Several extremely interesting cases were brought to him about this time, but he declined them all. Every morning he would rush at his letters, scrutinise them earnestly and then lay them down with a sigh.

But our patience was rewarded at last. On the Wednesday following Mrs Todd's visit, our landlady informed us that a person of the name of Eliza Dunn had called.

"*Enfin!*" cried Poirot. "But make her mount then! At once. Immediately."

Thus admonished, our landlady hurried out and returned a moment or two later, ushering in Miss Dunn. Our quarry was much as described: tall, stout, and eminently respectable.

"I came in answer to the advertisement," she explained. "I thought there must be some muddle or other, and that perhaps you didn't know I'd already got my legacy."

Poirot was studying her attentively. He drew forward a chair with a flourish.

"The truth of the matter is," he explained, "that your late mistress, Mrs Todd, was much concerned about you. She feared some accident might have befallen you."

Eliza Dunn seemed very much surprised.

"Didn't she get my letter then?"

"She got no word of any kind." He paused, and then said persuasively: "Recount to me the whole story, will you not?"

Eliza Dunn needed no encouragement. She plunged at once into a lengthy narrative.

"I was just coming home on Wednesday night and had nearly got to the house, when a gentleman stopped me. A tall gentleman he was, with a beard and a big hat. 'Miss Eliza Dunn?' he said. 'Yes,' I said. 'I've been inquiring for you at No. 88,' he said. 'They told me I might meet you coming along here. Miss Dunn, I have come from Australia specially to find you. Do you happen to know the maiden name of your maternal grandmother?' 'Jane Emmott,' I said. 'Exactly,' he said. 'Now, Miss Dunn, although you may never have heard of the fact, your grandmother had a great friend, Eliza Leech. This friend went to Australia where she married a very wealthy settler. Her two children died in infancy, and she inherited all her husband's property. She died a few months ago, and by her will you inherit a house in this country and a considerable sum of money.'

"You could have knocked me down with a feather," continued Miss Dunn. "For a minute, I was suspicious, and he must have seen it, for he smiled. 'Quite right to be on your guard, Miss Dunn,' he said. 'Here are my credentials.' He handed me a letter from some lawyers in Melbourne, Hurst and Crotchet, and a card. He was Mr Crotchet. 'There are one or two conditions,' he said. 'Our client was a little eccentric, you know. The bequest is conditional on your taking possession of the house (it is in Cumberland) before twelve o'clock tomorrow. The other condition is of no importance — it is merely a stipulation that you should not be in domestic service.' My face fell. 'Oh! Mr Crotchet,' I said. 'I'm a cook. Didn't they tell you at the house?' 'Dear, dear,' he said. 'I had no idea of such a thing. I thought you might possibly be a companion or governess there. This is very unfortunate — very unfortunate indeed.'

" 'Shall I have to lose all the money?' I said, anxious like. He thought for a minute or two. 'There are always ways of getting round the law, Miss Dunn,' he said at last. 'We lawyers know that. The way out here is for you to have left your employment this afternoon.' 'But my month?' I said. 'My dear Miss Dunn,' he said with a smile. 'You can leave an employer any minute by forfeiting a month's wages. Your mistress will understand in view of the circumstances. The difficulty is *time*! It is imperative that you should catch the 11.05 from King's Cross to the North. I can advance you ten pounds or so for the fare, and you can write a note at the station to your employer. I will take it to her myself and explain the whole circumstances.' I agreed, of course, and an hour later I was in the train, so flustered that I didn't know whether I was on my head or my heels. Indeed by the time I got to Carlisle, I was half inclined to think the whole thing was one of those confidence tricks you read about. But I went to the address he had given me — solicitors they were, and it was all right. A nice little house, and an income of three hundred a year. These lawyers knew very little, they'd just got a letter from a gentleman in London instructing them to hand over the house to me and £150 for the first six months. Mr Crotchet sent up my things to me, but there was no word from Missus. I supposed she was angry and grudged me my bit of luck. She kept back my box too, and sent my clothes in paper parcels. But there, of course if she never had my letter, she might think it a bit cool of me."

Poirot had listened attentively to this long history. Now he nodded his head as though completely satisfied.

"Thank you, Mademoiselle. There had been, as you say, a little muddle. Permit me to recompense you for your trouble." He handed her an envelope. "You return to Cumberland immediately? A little word in your ear. *Do not forget how to cook.* It is always useful to have something to fall back upon in case things go wrong."

"Credulous," he murmured, as our visitor departed, "but perhaps not more than most of her class." His face grew grave. "Come, Hastings, there is no time to be lost. Get a taxi while I write a note to Japp."

Poirot was waiting on the doorstep when I returned with the taxi.

"Where are we going?" I asked anxiously.

"First, to despatch this note by special messenger."

This was done, and reentering the taxi Poirot gave the address to the driver.

"88 Prince Albert Road, Clapham."

"So we are going there?"

"*Mais oui.* Though frankly I fear we shall be too late. Our bird will have flown, Hastings."

"Who is our bird?"

Poirot smiled.

"The inconspicuous Mr Simpson."

"What?" I exclaimed.

"Oh! come now, Hastings, do not tell me that all is not clear to you now!"

"The cook was got out of the way, I realise that," I said, slightly piqued. "But why? *Why* should Simpson wish to get her out of the house? Did she know something about him?"

"Nothing whatever."

"Well, then——"

"But he wanted something that she had."

"Money? The Australian legacy?"

"No, my friend — something quite different." He paused a moment and then said gravely: "*A battered tin trunk* . . ."

I looked sideways at him. His statement seemed so fantastic that I suspected him of pulling my leg, but he was perfectly grave and serious.

"Surely he could buy a trunk if he wanted one," I cried.

"He did not want a new trunk. He wanted a trunk of pedigree. A trunk of assured respectability."

"Look here, Poirot," I cried, "this really is a bit thick. You're pulling my leg."

He looked at me.

"You lack the brains and the imagination of Mr Simpson, Hastings. See here: On Wednesday evening, Simpson decoys away the cook. A printed card and a printed sheet of notepaper are simple matters to obtain, and he is willing to pay £150 and a year's house rent to assure the success of his plan. Miss Dunn does not recognise him — the beard and the hat and the slight colonial accent completely deceive her. That is the end of Wednesday — except for the trifling fact that Simpson has helped himself to fifty thousand pounds' worth of negotiable securities."

"*Simpson* — but it was Davis——"

"If you will kindly permit me to continue, Hastings! Simpson knows that the theft will be discovered on Thursday afternoon. He does not go to the bank on Thursday, but he lies in wait for Davis when he comes out to lunch. Perhaps he admits the theft and tells Davis he will return the securities to him — anyhow he succeeds in getting Davis to come to Clapham with him. It is the maid's day out, and Mrs Todd was at the

Sales, so there is no one in the house. When the theft is discovered and Davis is missing, the implication will be overwhelming. Davis is the thief! Mr Simpson will be perfectly safe, and can return to work on the morrow like the honest clerk they think him."

"And Davis?"

Poirot made an expressive gesture, and slowly shook his head.

"It seems too cold-blooded to be believed, and yet what other explanation can there be, *mon ami*. The one difficulty for a murderer is the disposal of the body — and Simpson had planned that out beforehand. I was struck at once by the fact that although Eliza Dunn obviously meant to return that night when she went out (witness her remark about the stewed peaches) *yet her trunk was already packed when they came for it*. It was Simpson who sent word to Carter Paterson to call on Friday and it was Simpson who corded up the box on Thursday afternoon. What suspicion could possibly arise? A maid leaves and sends for her box, it is labelled and addressed ready in her name, probably to a railway station within easy reach of London. On Saturday afternoon, Simpson, in his Australian disguise, claims it, he affixes a new label and address and redespatches it somewhere else, again 'to be left till called for'. When the authorities get suspicious, for excellent reasons, and open it, all that can be elicited will be that a bearded colonial despatched it from some junction near London. There will be nothing to connect it with 88 Prince Albert Road. Ah! here we are."

Poirot's prognostications had been correct. Simpson had left two days previously. But he was not to escape the consequences of his crime. By the aid of wireless, he was discovered on the *Olympia*, en route to America.

A tin trunk, addressed to Mr Henry Wintergreen, attracted the attention of railway officials at Glasgow. It was opened and found to contain the body of the unfortunate Davis.

Mrs Todd's cheque for a guinea was never cashed. Instead Poirot had it framed and hung on the wall of our sitting room.

"It is to me a little reminder, Hastings. Never to despise the trivial — the undignified. A disappearing domestic at one end — a cold-blooded murder at the other. To me, one of the most interesting of my cases."

Accident

"... And I tell you this — it's the same woman — not a doubt of it!"

Captain Haydock looked into the eager, vehement face of his friend and sighed. He wished Evans would not be so positive and so jubilant. In the course of a career spent at sea, the old sea captain had learned to leave things that did not concern him well alone. His friend, Evans, late CID* inspector, had a different philosophy of life. "Acting on information received——" had been his motto in early days, and he had improved upon it to the extent of finding out his own information. Inspector Evans had been a very smart, wide-awake officer, and had justly earned the promotion which had been his. Even now, when he had retired from the force, and had settled down in the country cottage of his dreams, his professional instinct was still active.

"Don't often forget a face," he reiterated complacently. "Mrs Anthony — yes, it's Mrs Anthony right enough. When you said Mrs Merrowdene — I knew her at once."

Captain Haydock stirred uneasily. The Merrowdenes were his nearest neighbours, barring Evans himself, and this identifying of Mrs Merrowdene with a former heroine of a *cause célèbre* distressed him.

"It's a long time ago," he said rather weakly.

"Nine years," said Evans, accurate as ever. "Nine years and three months. You remember the case?"

"In a vague sort of way."

"Anthony turned out to be an arsenic eater," said Evans, "so they acquitted her."

"Well, why shouldn't they?"

* CID: the Criminal Investigation Department of the British police

"No reason in the world. Only verdict they could give on the evidence. Absolutely correct."

"Then that's all right," said Haydock. "And I don't see what we're bothering about."

"Who's bothering?"

"I thought you were."

"Not at all."

"The thing's over and done with," summed up the captain. "If Mrs Merrowdene at one time of her life was unfortunate enough to be tried and acquitted for murder——"

"It's not usually considered unfortunate to be acquitted," put in Evans.

"You know what I mean," said Captain Haydock irritably. "If the poor lady has been through that harrowing experience, it's no business of ours to rake it up, is it?"

Evans did not answer.

"Come now, Evans. The lady was innocent — you've just said so."

"I didn't say she was innocent. I said she was acquitted."

"It's the same thing."

"Not always."

Captain Haydock, who had commenced to tap his pipe out against the side of his chair, stopped, and sat up with a very alert expression.

"Hallo — 'allo — 'allo," he said. "The wind's in that quarter, is it? You think she wasn't innocent?"

"I wouldn't say that. I just — don't know. Anthony was in the habit of taking arsenic. His wife got it for him. One day, by mistake, he takes far too much. Was the mistake his or his wife's? Nobody could tell, and the jury very properly gave her the benefit of the doubt. That's all quite right and I'm not finding fault with it. All the same — I'd like to *know*."

Captain Haydock transferred his attention to his pipe once more.

"Well," he said comfortably. "It's none of our business."

"I'm not so sure . . ."

"But surely——"

"Listen to me a minute. This man, Merrowdene — in his laboratory this evening, fiddling round with tests — you remember——"

"Yes. He mentioned Marsh's test for arsenic. Said *you* would know all about it — it was in *your* line — and chuckled. He wouldn't have said that if he'd thought for one moment——"

Evans interrupted him.

"You mean he wouldn't have said that if he *knew*. They've been married how long — six years you told me? I bet you anything he has no idea his wife is the once notorious Mrs Anthony."

"And he will certainly not know it from me," said Captain Haydock stiffly.

Evans paid no attention, but went on:

"You interrupted me just now. After Marsh's test, Merrowdene heated a substance in a test tube, the metallic residue he dissolved in water and then precipitated it by adding silver nitrate. That was a test for chlorates. A neat unassuming little test. But I chanced to read these words in a book that stood open on the table: 'H_2SO_4 decomposes chlorates with evolution of CL_4O_2. If heated, violent explosions occur; the mixture ought therefore to be kept cool and only very small quantities used.'"

Haydock stared at his friend.

"Well, what about it?"

"Just this. In my profession we've got tests too — tests for murder. There's adding up the facts — weighing them, dissecting the residue when you've allowed for prejudice and the general inaccuracy of witnesses. But there's another test of murder — one that is fairly accurate, but rather — dangerous! *A murderer is seldom content with one crime.* Give him time, and a lack of suspicion, and he'll commit another. You catch a man — has he murdered his wife or hasn't he? — perhaps the case isn't very black against him. Look into his past — if you find that he's had several wives — and that they've all died shall we say — rather curiously? — then you *know*! I'm not speaking *legally*, you understand. I'm speaking of *moral* certainty. Once you *know*, you can go ahead looking for evidence."

"Well?"

"I'm coming to the point. That's all right if there *is* a past to look into. But suppose you catch your murderer at his or her first crime? Then that test will be one from which you get no reaction. But suppose the prisoner was acquitted — starting life under another name. Will or will not the murderer repeat the crime?"

"That's a horrible idea!"

"Do you still say it's none of our business?"

"Yes, I do. You've no reason to think that Mrs Merrowdene is anything but a perfectly innocent woman."

The ex-inspector was silent for a moment. Then he said slowly:

"I told you that we looked into her past and found nothing. That's not quite true. There was a stepfather. As a girl of eighteen she had a fancy for some young man — and her stepfather exerted his authority to keep them apart. She and her stepfather went for a walk along a rather dangerous part of the cliff. There was an accident — the stepfather went too near the edge — it gave way, and he went over and was killed."

"You don't think——"

"It was an accident. *Accident!* Anthony's overdose of arsenic was an accident. She'd never have been tried if it hadn't transpired that there was another man — he sheered off, by the way. Looked as though he weren't satisfied even if the jury were. I tell you, Haydock, where that woman is concerned I'm afraid of another — accident!"

The old captain shrugged his shoulders.

"It's been nine years since that affair. Why should there be another 'accident', as you call it, now?"

"I didn't say now. I said some day or other. If the necessary motive arose."

Captain Haydock shrugged his shoulders.

"Well, I don't know how you're going to guard against that."

"Neither do I," said Evans ruefully.

"I should leave well alone," said Captain Haydock. "No good ever came of butting into other people's affairs."

But that advice was not palatable to the ex-inspector. He was a man of patience but determination. Taking leave of his friend, he sauntered down to the village, revolving in his mind the possibilities of some kind of successful action.

Turning into the post office to buy some stamps, he ran into the object of his solicitude, George Merrowdene. The ex-chemistry professor was a small dreamy-looking man, gentle and kindly in manner, and usually completely absent-minded. He recognised the other and greeted him amicably, stooping to recover the letters that the impact had caused him to drop on the ground. Evans stooped also and, more rapid in his movements than the other, secured them first, handing them back to their owner with an apology.

He glanced down at them in doing so, and the address on the topmost suddenly awakened all his suspicions anew. It bore the name of a well-known insurance firm.

Instantly his mind was made up. The guileless George Merrowdene hardly realised how it came about that he and the ex-inspector were strolling down the village together, and still less could he have said how it came about that the conversation should come round to the subject of life insurance.

Evans had no difficulty in attaining his object. Merrowdene of his own accord volunteered the information that he had just insured his life for his wife's benefit, and asked Evans's opinion of the company in question.

"I made some rather unwise investments," he explained. "As a result my income has diminished. If anything were to happen to me, my wife would be left very badly off. This insurance will put things right."

"She didn't object to the idea?" inquired Evans casually. "Some ladies do, you know. Feel it's unlucky — that sort of thing."

"Oh, Margaret is very practical," said Merrowdene, smiling. "Not at all superstitious. In fact, I believe it was her idea originally. She didn't like my being so worried."

Evans had got the information he wanted. He left the other shortly afterwards, and his lips were set in a grim line. The late Mr Anthony had insured his life in his wife's favour a few weeks before his death.

Accustomed to rely on his instincts, he was perfectly sure in his own mind. But how to act was another matter. He wanted, not to arrest a criminal red-handed, but to prevent a crime being committed, and that was a very different and a very much more difficult thing.

All day he was very thoughtful. There was a Primrose League Fete that afternoon held in the grounds of the local squire, and he went to it, indulging in the penny dip, guessing the weight of a pig, and shying at coconuts all with the same look of abstracted concentration on his face. He even indulged in half a crown's worth of Zara, the Crystal Gazer, smiling a little to himself as he did so, remembering his own activities against fortune-tellers in his official days.

He did not pay very much heed to her sing-song droning voice — till the end of a sentence held his attention.

". . . And you will very shortly — very shortly indeed — be engaged on a matter of life or death . . . Life or death to one person."

"Eh — what's that?" he asked abruptly.

"A decision — you have a decision to make. You must be very careful — very, very careful . . . If you were to make a mistake — the smallest mistake——"

"Yes?"

The fortune-teller shivered. Inspector Evans knew it was all nonsense, but he was nevertheless impressed.

"I warn you — *you must not make a mistake*. If you do, I see the result clearly — a death . . ."

Odd, damned odd. A death. Fancy her lighting upon that!

"If I make a mistake a death will result? Is that it?"

"Yes."

"In that case," said Evans, rising to his feet and handing over half a crown, "I mustn't make a mistake, eh?"

He spoke lightly enough, but as he went out of the tent, his jaw set determinedly. Easy to say — not so easy to be sure of doing. He mustn't make a slip. A life, a valuable human life depended on it.

And there was no one to help him. He looked across at the figure of his friend Haydock in the distance. No help there. "Leave things alone," was Haydock's motto. And that wouldn't do here.

Haydock was talking to a woman. She moved away from him and came towards Evans and the inspector recognised her. It was Mrs Merrowdene. On an impulse he put himself deliberately in her path.

Mrs Merrowdene was rather a fine-looking woman. She had a broad serene brow, very beautiful brown eyes, and a placid expression. She had the look of an Italian madonna which she heightened by parting her hair in the middle and looping it over her ears. She had a deep rather sleepy voice.

She smiled up at Evans, a contented welcoming smile.

"I thought it was you, Mrs Anthony — I mean Mrs Merrowdene," he said glibly.

He made the slip deliberately, watching her without seeming to do so. He saw her eyes widen, heard the quick intake of her breath. But her eyes did not falter. She gazed at him steadily and proudly.

"I was looking for my husband," she said quietly. "Have you seen him anywhere about?"

"He was over in that direction when I last saw him."

They went side by side in the direction indicated, chatting quietly and pleasantly. The inspector felt his admiration mounting. What a woman! What self-command. What wonderful poise. A remarkable woman — and a very dangerous one. He felt sure — a very dangerous one.

He still felt very uneasy, though he was satisfied with his initial step. He had let her know that he recognised her. That would put her on her guard. She would not dare attempt anything rash. There was the question of Merrowdene. If he could be warned . . .

They found the little man absently contemplating a china doll which had fallen to his share in the penny dip. His wife suggested going home and he agreed eagerly. Mrs Merrowdene turned to the inspector:

"Won't you come back with us and have a quiet cup of tea, Mr Evans?"

Was there a faint note of challenge in her voice? He thought there was.

"Thank you, Mrs Merrowdene. I should like to very much."

They walked there, talking together of pleasant ordinary things. The sun shone, a breeze blew gently, everything around them was pleasant and ordinary.

Their maid was out at the fete, Mrs Merrowdene explained, when they arrived at the charming old-world cottage. She went into her room to remove her hat, returning to set out tea and boil the kettle on a little silver lamp. From a shelf near the fireplace she took three small bowls and saucers.

"We have some very special Chinese tea," she explained. "And we always drink it in the Chinese manner — out of bowls, not cups."

She broke off, peered into a cup and exchanged it for another with an exclamation of annoyance.

"George — it's too bad of you. You've been taking these bowls again."

"I'm sorry, dear," said the professor apologetically. "They're such a convenient size. The ones I ordered haven't come."

"One of these days you'll poison us all," said his wife with a half-laugh. "Mary finds them in the laboratory and brings them back here, and never troubles to wash them out unless they've anything very noticeable in them. Why, you were using one of them for potassium cyanide the other day. Really, George, it's frightfully dangerous."

Merrowdene looked a little irritated.

"Mary's no business to remove things from the laboratory. She's not to touch anything there."

"But we often leave our teacups there after tea. How is she to know? Be reasonable, dear."

The professor went into his laboratory, murmuring to himself, and with a smile Mrs Merrowdene poured boiling water on the tea and blew out the flame of the little silver lamp.

Evans was puzzled. Yet a glimmering of light penetrated to him. For some reason or other, Mrs Merrowdene was showing her hand. Was this to be the "accident"? Was she speaking of all this so as deliberately to prepare her alibi beforehand? So that when, one day, the "accident" happened, he would be forced to give evidence in her favour. Stupid of her, if so, because before that——

Suddenly he drew in his breath. She had poured the tea into the three bowls. One she set before him, one before herself, the other she placed on a little table by the fire near the chair her husband usually sat in, and it was as she placed this last one on the table that a little strange smile curved round her lips. It was the smile that did it.

He *knew*!

A remarkable woman — a dangerous woman. No waiting — no preparation. This afternoon — this very afternoon — with him here as witness. The boldness of it took his breath away.

It was clever — it was damnably clever. He would be able to prove nothing. She counted on his not suspecting — simply because it was "so soon". A woman of lightning rapidity of thought and action.

He drew a deep breath and leaned forward.

"Mrs Merrowdene, I'm a man of queer whims. Will you be very kind and indulge me in one of them?"

She looked inquiring but unsuspicious.

He rose, took the bowl from in front of her and crossed to the little table where he substituted it for the other. This other he brought back and placed in front of her.

"I want to see you drink this."

Her eyes met his. They were steady, unfathomable. The colour slowly drained from her face.

She stretched out her hand, raised the cup. He held his breath. Supposing all along he had made a mistake.

She raised it to her lips — at the last moment, with a shudder, she leant forward and quickly poured it into a pot containing a fern. Then she sat back and gazed at him defiantly.

He drew a long sigh of relief, and sat down again.

"Well?" she said.

Her voice had altered. It was slightly mocking — defiant.

He answered her soberly and quietly:

"You are a very clever woman, Mrs Merrowdene. I think you understand me. There must be no — repetition. You know what I mean?"

"I know what you mean."

Her voice was even, devoid of expression. He nodded his head, satisfied. She was a clever woman, and she didn't want to be hanged.

"To your long life and to that of your husband," he said significantly, and raised his tea to his lips.

Then his face changed. It contorted horribly . . . he tried to rise — to cry out . . . His body stiffened — his face went purple. He fell back sprawling over his chair — his limbs convulsed.

Mrs Merrowdene leaned forward, watching him. A little smile crossed her lips. She spoke to him — very softly and gently.

"You made a mistake, Mr Evans. You thought I wanted to kill George . . . How stupid of you — how very stupid."

She sat there a minute longer looking at the dead man, the third man who had threatened to cross her path and separate her from the man she loved.

Her smile broadened. She looked more than ever like a madonna. Then she raised her voice and called:

"George, George! . . . Oh, do come here! I'm afraid there's been the most dreadful accident . . . Poor Mr Evans . . ."

The Lernean Hydra

I

Hercule Poirot looked encouragingly at the man seated opposite him.

Dr Charles Oldfield was a man of perhaps forty. He had fair hair slightly grey at the temples and blue eyes that held a worried expression. He stooped a little and his manner was a trifle hesitant. Moreover, he seemed to find difficulty in coming to the point.

He said, stammering slightly:

"I've come to you, M. Poirot, with rather an odd request. And now that I'm here, I'm inclined to funk the whole thing. Because, as I see very well now, it's the sort of thing that no one can possibly do anything about."

Hercule Poirot murmured:

"As to that, you must let me judge."

Oldfield muttered:

"I don't know why I thought that perhaps——"

He broke off.

Hercule Poirot finished the sentence:

"That perhaps I could help you? *Eh bien*, perhaps I can. Tell me your problem."

Oldfield straightened himself. Poirot noted anew how haggard the man looked.

Oldfield said, and his voice had a note of hopelessness in it:

"You see, it isn't any good going to the police . . . They can't do anything. And yet — every day it's getting worse and worse. I — I don't know what to do . . ."

"*What* is getting worse?"

"The rumours . . . Oh, it's quite simple, M. Poirot. Just a little over a year ago, my wife died. She had been an invalid for some years. They are saying, everyone is saying, *that I killed her* — that I poisoned her!"

"Aha," said Poirot. "And did you poison her?"

"M. Poirot!" Dr Oldfield sprang to his feet.

"Calm yourself," said Hercule Poirot. "And sit down again. We will take it, then, that you did *not* poison your wife. But your practice, I imagine, is situated in a country district——"

"Yes. Market Loughborough — in Berkshire. I have always realised that it was the kind of place where people gossiped a good deal, but I never imagined that it could reach the lengths it has done." He drew his chair a little forward. "M. Poirot, you have no idea of what I have gone through. At first I had no inkling of what was going on. I did notice that people seemed less friendly, that there was a tendency to avoid me — but I put it down to — to the fact of my recent bereavement. Then it became more marked. In the street, even, people will cross the road to avoid speaking to me. My practice is falling off. Wherever I go I am conscious of lowered voices, of unfriendly eyes that watch me whilst malicious tongues whisper their deadly poison. I have had one or two letters — vile things."

He paused — and then went on:

"And — and *I don't know what to do about it*. I don't know how to fight this — this vile network of lies and suspicion. How can one refute what is never said openly to your face? I am powerless — trapped — and slowly and mercilessly being destroyed."

Poirot nodded his head thoughtfully. He said:

"Yes. Rumour is indeed the nine-headed Hydra of Lernea which cannot be exterminated because as fast as one head is cropped off two grow in its place."

Dr Oldfield said: "That's just it. There's nothing I can do — *nothing*! I came to you as a last resort — but I don't suppose for a minute that there is anything you can do either."

Hercule Poirot was silent for a minute or two. Then he said:

"I am not so sure. Your problem interests me, Doctor Oldfield. I should like to try my hand at destroying the many-headed monster. First of all, tell me a little more about the circumstances which gave rise to this malicious gossip. Your wife died, you say, just over a year ago. What was the cause of death?"

"Gastric ulcer."

"Was there an autopsy?"

"No. She had been suffering from gastric trouble over a considerable period."

Poirot nodded.

"And the symptoms of gastric inflammation and of arsenical poisoning are closely alike — a fact which everybody knows nowadays. Within the last ten years there have been at least four sensational murder cases in each of which the victim has been buried without suspicion with a certificate of gastric disorder. Was your wife older or younger than yourself?"

"She was five years older."

"How long had you been married?"

"Fifteen years."

"Did she leave any property?"

"Yes. She was a fairly well-to-do woman. She left, roughly, about thirty thousand pounds."

"A very useful sum. It was left to you?"

"Yes."

"Were you and your wife on good terms?"

"Certainly."

"No quarrels? No scenes?"

"Well——" Charles Oldfield hesitated. "My wife was what might be termed a difficult woman. She was an invalid and very concerned over her health and inclined, therefore, to be fretful and difficult to please. There were days when nothing I could do was right."

Poirot nodded. He said:

"Ah yes, I know the type. She would complain, possibly, that she was neglected, unappreciated — that her husband was tired of her and would be glad when she was dead."

Oldfield's face registered the truth of Poirot's surmise. He said with a wry smile:

"You've got it exactly!"

Poirot went on:

"Did she have a hospital nurse to attend on her? Or a companion? Or a devoted maid?"

"A nurse-companion. A very sensible and competent woman. I really don't think she would talk."

"Even the sensible and the competent have been given tongues by *le bon Dieu* — and they do not always employ their tongues wisely. I have no doubt that the nurse-companion talked, that the servants talked, that everyone talked! You have all the materials there for the starting of a very enjoyable village scandal. Now I will ask you one thing more. *Who is the lady?*"

"I don't understand." Dr Oldfield flushed angrily.

Poirot said gently:

"I think you do. I am asking you who the lady is with whom your name has been coupled."

Dr Oldfield rose to his feet. His face was stiff and cold. He said:

"There is no 'lady in the case'. I'm sorry, M. Poirot, to have taken up so much of your time."

He went towards the door.

Hercule Poirot said:

"I regret it also. Your case interests me. I would like to have helped you. But I cannot do anything unless I am told the whole truth."

"I have told you the truth."

"No . . ."

Dr Oldfield stopped. He wheeled round.

"Why do you insist that there is a woman concerned in this?"

"*Mon cher docteur!* Do you not think I know the female mentality? The village gossip, it is based always, always, on the relations of the sexes. If a man poisons his wife in order to travel to the North Pole or to enjoy the peace of a bachelor existence — it would not interest his fellow-villagers for a minute! It is because they are convinced that the murder has been committed in order *that the man may marry another woman* that the talk grows and spreads. That is elemental psychology."

Oldfield said irritably:

"I'm not responsible for what a pack of damned gossiping busybodies think!"

"Of course you are not."

Poirot went on:

"So you might as well come back and sit down and give me the answer to the question I asked you just now."

Slowly, almost reluctantly, Oldfield came back and resumed his seat.

He said, colouring up to his eyebrows:

"I suppose it's possible that they've been saying things about Miss Moncrieffe. Jean Moncrieffe is my dispenser, a very fine girl indeed."

"How long has she worked for you?"

"For three years."

"Did your wife like her?"

"Er — well, no, not exactly."

"She was jealous?"

"It was absurd!"

Poirot smiled.

He said:

"The jealousy of wives is proverbial. But I will tell you something. In my experience jealousy, however far-fetched and extravagant it may seem, is nearly always based on *reality*. There is a saying, is there not, that the customer is always right? Well, the same is true of the jealous husband or wife. However little *concrete* evidence there may be, *fundamentally* they are always right."

Dr Oldfield said robustly:

"Nonsense. I've never said anything to Jean Moncrieffe that my wife couldn't have overheard."

"That, perhaps. But it does not alter the truth of what I said." Hercule Poirot leaned forward. His voice was urgent, compelling. "Doctor Oldfield, I am going to do my utmost in this case. But I must have from you the most absolute frankness without regard to conventional appearances or to your own feelings. It is true, is it not, that you had ceased to care for your wife for some time before she died?"

Oldfield was silent for a minute or two. Then he said:

"This business is killing me. I must have hope. Somehow or other I feel that you will be able to do something for me. I will be honest with you, M. Poirot. I did not care deeply for my wife. I made her, I think, a good husband, but I was never really in love with her."

"And this girl, Jean?"

The perspiration came out in a fine dew on the doctor's forehead. He said:

"I — I should have asked her to marry me before now if it weren't for all this scandal and talk."

Poirot sat back in his chair. He said:

"Now at last we have come to the true facts! *Eh bien*, Doctor Oldfield, I will take up your case. But remember this — it is the *truth* that I shall seek out."

Oldfield said bitterly:

"It isn't the truth that's going to hurt me!"

He hesitated and said:

"You know, I've contemplated the possibility of an action for slander! If I could pin anyone down to a definite accusation — surely then I should be vindicated? At least, sometimes I think so . . . At other times I think it would only make things worse — give bigger publicity to the whole thing and have people saying: '*It mayn't have been proved but there's no smoke without fire.*'"

He looked at Poirot.

"Tell me, honestly, is there *any* way out of this nightmare?"

"There is always a way," said Hercule Poirot.

II

"We are going into the country, Georges," said Hercule Poirot to his valet.

"Indeed, sir?" said the imperturbable George.

"And the purpose of our journey is to destroy a monster with nine heads."

"Really, sir? Something after the style of the Loch Ness Monster?"*

"Less tangible than that. I did not refer to a flesh and blood animal, Georges."

"I misunderstood you, sir."

"It would be easier if it were one. There is nothing so intangible, so difficult to pin down, as the source of a rumour."

"Oh yes, indeed, sir. It's difficult to know how a thing starts sometimes."

"Exactly."

Hercule Poirot did not put up at Dr Oldfield's house. He went instead to the local inn. The morning after his arrival, he had his first interview with Jean Moncrieffe.

She was a tall girl with copper-coloured hair and steady blue eyes. She

*Loch Ness Monster: a large creature which is said by some to live in a Scottish lake, although its existence has never been proved

had about her a watchful look, as of one who is upon her guard.

She said:

"So Doctor Oldfield did go to you . . . I knew he was thinking about it."

There was a lack of enthusiasm in her tone.

Poirot said:

"And you did not approve?"

Her eyes met his. She said coldly:

"What can you do?"

Poirot said quietly:

"There might be a way of tackling the situation."

"What way?" She threw the words at him scornfully. "Do you mean to go round to all the whispering old women and say: '*Really, please, you must stop talking like this. It's so bad for poor Doctor Oldfield.*' And they'd answer you and say: 'Of course, *I* have never believed the story!' That's the worst of the whole thing — they don't say: 'My dear, has it ever occurred to you that perhaps Mrs Oldfield's death wasn't quite what it seemed?' No, they say: 'My dear, of course I *don't* believe that story about Doctor Oldfield and his wife. I'm *sure* he wouldn't do such a thing, though it's true that he *did* neglect her just a little perhaps and I don't think, really, it's quite *wise* to have quite a young girl as his dispenser — of course, I'm not saying for a minute that there was anything *wrong* between them. Oh no, I'm sure it was *quite* all right . . .'" She stopped. Her face was flushed and her breath came rather fast.

Hercule Poirot said:

"You seem to know very well just what is being said."

Her mouth closed sharply. She said bitterly:

"I know all right!"

"And what is your own solution?"

Jean Moncrieffe said:

"The best thing for him to do is to sell his practice and start again somewhere else."

"Don't you think the story might follow him?"

She shrugged her shoulders.

"He must risk that."

Poirot was silent for a minute or two. Then he said:

"Are you going to marry Doctor Oldfield, Miss Moncrieffe?"

She displayed no surprise at the question. She said shortly:

"He hasn't asked me to marry him."

"Why not?"

Her blue eyes met his and flickered for a second. Then she said:

"Because I've choked him off."

"Ah, what a blessing to find someone who can be frank!"

"I will be as frank as you please. When I realised that people were saying that Charles had got rid of his wife in order to marry me, it seemed to me that if we *did* marry it would just put the lid on things. I hoped that if there appeared to be no question of marriage between us, the silly scandal might die down."

"But it hasn't?"

"No, it hasn't."

"Surely," said Hercule Poirot, "that is a little odd?"

Jean said bitterly:

"They haven't got much to amuse them down here."

Poirot asked:

"Do you *want* to marry Charles Oldfield?"

The girl answered coolly enough.

"Yes, I do. I wanted to almost as soon as I met him."

"Then his wife's death was very convenient for you?"

Jean Moncrieffe said:

"Mrs Oldfield was a singularly unpleasant woman. Frankly, I was delighted when she died."

"Yes," said Poirot. "You are certainly frank!"

She gave the same scornful smile.

Poirot said:

"I have a suggestion to make."

"Yes?"

"Drastic means are required here. I suggest that somebody — possibly yourself — might write to the Home Office."*

"What on earth do you mean?"

"I mean that the best way of disposing of this story once and for all is to get the body exhumed and an autopsy performed."

She took a step back from him. Her lips opened, then shut again. Poirot watched her.

"Well, Mademoiselle?" he said at last.

Jean Moncrieffe said quietly:

"I don't agree with you."

"But why not? Surely a verdict of death from natural causes would silence all tongues?"

"*If* you got that verdict, yes."

"Do you know what you are suggesting, Mademoiselle?"

Jean Moncrieffe said impatiently:

"I know what I'm talking about. You're thinking of arsenic poisoning — you could prove that she was not poisoned by arsenic. But there are other poisons — the vegetable alkaloids. After a year, I doubt if you'd find any traces of them even if they had been used. And I know what these official analyst people are like. They might return a noncommittal verdict saying that there was nothing to show what caused death — and then the tongues would wag faster than ever!"

Hercule Poirot was silent for a minute or two, then he said:

"Who in your opinion is the most inveterate talker in the village?"

---

*Home Office: the British government department which deals with internal affairs (permission to dig up a dead body must be obtained from the department)

The girl considered. She said at last:

"I really think old Miss Leatheran is the worst cat of the lot."

"Ah! would it be possible for you to introduce me to Miss Leatheran — in a casual manner if possible?"

"Nothing could be easier. All the old tabbies are prowling about doing their shopping at this time of the morning. We've only got to walk down the main street."

As Jean had said, there was no difficulty about the procedure. Outside the post office, Jean stopped and spoke to a tall, thin, middle-aged woman with a long nose and sharp inquisitive eyes.

"Good morning, Miss Leatheran."

"Good morning, Jean. Such a lovely day, is it not?"

The sharp eyes ranged inquisitively over Jean Moncrieffe's companion. Jean said:

"Let me introduce M. Poirot, who is staying down here for a few days."

III

Nibbling delicately at a scone and balancing a cup of tea on his knee, Hercule Poirot allowed himself to become confidential with his hostess. Miss Leatheran had been kind enough to ask him to tea and had thereupon made it her business to find out exactly what this exotic little foreigner was doing in their midst.

For some time he parried her thrusts with dexterity — thereby whetting her appetite. Then, when he judged the moment ripe, he leant forward:

"Ah, Miss Leatheran," he said. "I can see that you are too clever for me! You have guessed my secret. I am down here at the request of the Home Office. But please," he lowered his voice, *"keep this information to yourself."*

"Of course — of course——" Miss Leatheran was flattered — thrilled to the core. "The Home Office — you don't mean — *not* poor Mrs Oldfield?"

Poirot nodded his head slowly several times.

"We-ell!" Miss Leatheran breathed into that one word a whole gamut of pleasurable emotion.

Poirot said:

"It is a delicate matter, you understand. I have been ordered to report whether there is or is not a sufficient case for exhumation."

Miss Leatheran exclaimed:

"You are going to dig the poor thing up. How terrible!"

If she had said "how splendid" instead of "how terrible" the words would have suited her tone of voice better.

"What is your own opinion, Miss Leatheran?"

"Well, of course, M. Poirot, there has been a lot of *talk*. But I never listen to *talk*. There is always so *much* unreliable gossip going about. There is no doubt that Doctor Oldfield has been very odd in his manner ever since it happened, but as I have said repeatedly we surely need not put that down to a *guilty conscience*. It might be just grief. Not, of course, that he and his wife were on really affectionate terms. That I *do* know — on *first-hand authority*. Nurse Harrison, who was with Mrs Oldfield for three or four years up to the time of her death, has admitted *that* much. And I have always felt, you know, that Nurse Harrison *had her suspicions* — not that she ever *said* anything, but one can *tell*, can't one, from a person's manner?"

Poirot said sadly:

"One has so little to go upon."

"Yes, I know, but of course, M. Poirot, if the body is exhumed then you will *know*."

"Yes," said Poirot, "then we will know."

"There have been cases like it before, of course," said Miss Leatheran, her nose twitching with pleasurable excitement. "Armstrong, for instance, and that other man — I can't remember his name — and then Crippen, of course. I've always wondered if Ethel Le Neve was in it with him or not. Of course, Jean Moncrieffe is a very nice girl, I'm sure . . . I wouldn't like to say she led him on exactly — but men do get rather *silly* about girls, don't they? And, of course, they *were* thrown very much together!"

Poirot did not speak. He looked at her with an innocent expression of inquiry calculated to produce a further spate of conversation. Inwardly he amused himself by counting the number of times the words "of course" occurred.

"And, of course, with a post-mortem and all that, so much would be bound to come out, wouldn't it? Servants and all that. Servants always know so much, don't they? And, of course, it's quite impossible to keep them from gossiping, isn't it? The Oldfields' Beatrice was dismissed almost immediately after the funeral — and I've always thought that was *odd* — especially with the difficulty of getting maids nowadays. It looks as though Doctor Oldfield was afraid she might *know* something."

"It certainly seems as though there were grounds for an inquiry," said Poirot solemnly.

Miss Leatheran gave a little shiver of reluctance.

"One does so shrink from the idea," she said. "Our dear quiet little village — dragged into the newspapers — all the *publicity*!"

"It appals you?" asked Poirot.

"It does a little. I'm old-fashioned, you know."

"And, as you say, it is probably nothing but gossip!"

"Well — I wouldn't like conscientiously to say *that*. You know, I do think it's so true — the saying that there's no smoke without fire."

"I myself was thinking exactly the same thing," said Poirot.

He rose.

"I can trust your discretion, Mademoiselle?"

"Oh, *of course*! I shall not say a *word* to *anybody*."

Poirot smiled and took his leave.

On the doorstep he said to the little maid who handed him his hat and coat:

"I am down here to inquire into the circumstances of Mrs Oldfield's death, but I shall be obliged if you will keep that strictly to yourself."

Miss Leatheran's Gladys nearly fell backward into the umbrella stand. She breathed excitedly:

"Oh sir, then the doctor *did* do her in?"

"You've thought so for some time, haven't you?"

"Well, sir, it wasn't *me*. It was Beatrice. She was up there when Mrs Oldfield died."

"And she thought there had been" — Poirot selected the melodramatic words deliberately — "'foul play'?"

Gladys nodded excitedly.

"Yes, she did. And she said so did Nurse that was up there, Nurse Harrison. Ever so fond of Mrs Oldfield Nurse was, and ever so distressed when she died, and Beatrice always said as how Nurse Harrison knew something about it because she turned right round against the doctor afterwards and she wouldn't have done that unless there was something wrong, would she?"

"Where is Nurse Harrison now?"

"She looks after old Miss Bristow — down at the end of the village. You can't miss it. It's got pillars and a porch."

IV

It was a very short time afterwards that Hercule Poirot found himself sitting opposite to the woman who certainly must know more about the circumstances that had given rise to the rumours than anyone else.

Nurse Harrison was a still-handsome woman nearing forty. She had the calm serene features of a madonna with big sympathetic dark eyes. She listened to him patiently and attentively. Then she said slowly:

"Yes, I know that there are these unpleasant stories going about. I have done what I could to stop them, but it's hopeless. People like the excitement, you know."

Poirot said:

"But there must have been *something* to give rise to these rumours?"

He noted that her expression of distress deepened. But she merely shook her head perplexedly.

"Perhaps," Poirot suggested, "Doctor Oldfield and his wife did not get on well together and it was that that started the rumour?"

Nurse Harrison shook her head decidedly.

"Oh no, Doctor Oldfield was always extremely kind and patient with his wife."

"He was really very fond of her?"

She hesitated.

"No — I would not quite say that. Mrs Oldfield was a very difficult woman, not easy to please and making constant demands for sympathy and attention which were not always justified."

"You mean," said Poirot, "that she exaggerated her condition?"

The nurse nodded.

"Yes — her bad health was largely a matter of her own imagination."

"And yet," said Poirot gravely, "*she died* . . ."

"Oh, I know — I know . . ."

He watched her for a minute or two; her troubled perplexity — her palpable uncertainty.

He said: "I think — I am sure — that you *do* know what first gave rise to all these stories."

Nurse Harrison flushed.

She said:

"Well — I could, perhaps, make a guess. I believe it was the maid,

Beatrice, who started all these rumours and I think I know what put it into her head."

"Yes?"

Nurse Harrison said rather incoherently:

"You see, it was something I happened to overhear — a scrap of conversation between Doctor Oldfield and Miss Moncrieffe — and I'm pretty certain Beatrice overheard it too, only I don't suppose she'd ever admit it."

"What was this conversation?"

Nurse Harrison paused for a minute as though to test the accuracy of her memory, then she said:

"It was about three weeks before the last attack that killed Mrs Oldfield. They were in the dining room. I was coming down the stairs when I heard Jean Moncrieffe say:

"'How much longer will it be? I can't bear to wait much longer.'

"And the doctor answered her:

"'Not much longer now, darling, I swear it.' And she said again:

"'I can't bear this waiting. You do think it will be all right, don't you?' And he said: 'Of course. Nothing can go wrong. This time next year we'll be married.'"

She paused.

"That was the very first inkling I'd had, M. Poirot, that there was anything between the doctor and Miss Moncrieffe. Of course I knew he admired her and that they were very good friends, but nothing more. I went back up the stairs again — it had given me quite a shock — but I did notice that the kitchen door was open and I've thought since that Beatrice must have been listening. And you can see, can't you, that the way they were talking could be taken two ways? It might just mean that the doctor knew his wife was very ill and couldn't live much longer — and I've no doubt that that was the way he meant it — but to anyone like Beatrice it might sound differently — it might look as though the doctor and Jean Moncrieffe were — well — were definitely planning to do away with Mrs Oldfield."

"But *you* don't think so, yourself?"

"No — no, of course not . . ."

Poirot looked at her searchingly. He said:

"Nurse Harrison, is there something more that you know? Something that you haven't told me?"

She flushed and said violently:

"No. No. Certainly not. What could there be?"

"I do not know. But I thought that there might be — something?"

She shook her head. The old troubled look had come back.

Hercule Poirot said: "It is possible that the Home Office may order an exhumation of Mrs Oldfield's body."

"Oh no!" Nurse Harrison was horrified. "What a horrible thing!"

"You think it would be a pity?"

"I think it would be *dreadful*! Think of the talk it would create! It would be terrible — quite terrible for poor Doctor Oldfield."

"You don't think that it might really be a good thing for him?"

"How do you mean?"

Poirot said: "If he is innocent — his innocence will be proved."

He broke off. He watched the thought take root in Nurse Harrison's mind, saw her frown perplexedly, and then saw her brow clear.

She took a deep breath and looked at him.

"I hadn't thought of that," she said simply. "Of course, it is the only thing to be done."

There were a series of thumps on the floor overhead. Nurse Harrison jumped up.

"It's my old lady, Miss Bristow. She's woken up from her rest. I must go and get her comfortable before her tea is brought to her and I go out for my walk. Yes, M. Poirot, I think you are quite right. An autopsy will settle the business once and for all. It will scotch the whole thing and all these dreadful rumours against poor Doctor Oldfield will die down."

She shook hands and hurried out of the room.

V

Hercule Poirot walked along to the post office and put through a call to London.

The voice at the other end was petulant.

"*Must* you go nosing out these things, my dear Poirot? Are you *sure* it's a case for us? You know what these country town rumours usually amount to — just nothing at all."

"This," said Hercule Poirot, "is a special case."

"Oh well — if you say so. You have such a tiresome habit of being right. But if it's all a mare's nest we shan't be pleased with you, you know."

Hercule Poirot smiled to himself. He murmured:

"No, *I* shall be the one who is pleased."

"What's that you say? Can't hear."

"Nothing. Nothing at all."

He rang off.

Emerging into the post office he leaned across the counter. He said in his most engaging tones:

"Can you by any chance tell me, Madame, where the maid who was formerly with Doctor Oldfield — Beatrice her Christian name was — now resides?"

"Beatrice King? She's had two places since then. She's with Mrs Marley over the Bank now."

Poirot thanked her, bought two postcards, a book of stamps, and a piece of local pottery. During the purchase, he contrived to bring the death of the late Mrs Oldfield into the conversation. He was quick to note the peculiar furtive expression that stole across the postmistress's face. She said:

"Very sudden, wasn't it? It's made a lot of talk as you may have heard."

A gleam of interest came into her eyes as she asked:

"Maybe that's what you'd be wanting to see Beatrice King for? We all thought it odd the way she was got out of there all of a sudden. Somebody thought she knew something — and *maybe she did*. She's dropped some pretty broad hints."

Beatrice King was a short rather sly-looking girl with adenoids. She presented an appearance of stolid stupidity but her eyes were more intelligent than her manner would have led one to expect. It seemed, however, that there was nothing to be got out of Beatrice King. She repeated:

"I don't know nothing about anything . . . It's not for me to say what went on up there . . . I don't know what you mean by overhearing a conversation between the doctor and Miss Moncrieffe. I'm not one to go listening at doors, and you've no right to say I did. I don't know nothing."

Poirot said:

"Have you ever heard of poisoning by arsenic?"

A flicker of quick furtive interest came into the girl's sullen face. She said:

"So *that's* what it was in the medicine bottle?"

"What medicine bottle?"

Beatrice said:

"One of the bottles of medicine what that Miss Moncrieffe made up for the Missus. Nurse was all upset — I could see that. Tasted it, she did, and smelt it, and then poured it away down the sink and filled up the bottle with plain water from the tap. It was white medicine like water, anyway. And once, when Miss Moncrieffe took up a pot of tea to the Missus, Nurse brought it down again and made it fresh — said it hadn't been made with boiling water, but that was just my eye, that was! I thought it was just the sort of fussing way nurses have at the time — but

I dunno — it may have been more than that."

Poirot nodded. He said:

"Did you like Miss Moncrieffe, Beatrice?"

"I didn't mind her . . . A bit standoffish. Of course, I always knew as she was sweet on the doctor. You'd only to see the way she looked at him."

Again Poirot nodded his head. He went back to the inn. There he gave certain instructions to George.

VI

Dr Alan Garcia, the Home Office Analyst, rubbed his hands and twinkled at Hercule Poirot. He said:

"Well, this suits you, M. Poirot, I suppose? The man who's always right."

Poirot said:

"You are too kind."

"What put you on to it? Gossip?"

"As you say — enter Rumour, painted full of tongues."

The following day Poirot once more took a train to Market Loughborough.

Market Loughborough was buzzing like a beehive. It had buzzed mildly ever since the exhumation proceedings.

Now that the findings of the autopsy had leaked out, excitement had reached fever heat.

Poirot had been at the inn for about an hour and had just finished a hearty lunch of steak and kidney pudding washed down by beer when word was brought to him that a lady was waiting to see him.

It was Nurse Harrison. Her face was white and haggard.

She came straight to Poirot.

"Is this true? Is this really true, M. Poirot?"

He put her gently into a chair.

"Yes. More than sufficient arsenic to cause death has been found."

Nurse Harrison cried:

"I never thought — I never for one moment thought——" and burst into tears.

Poirot said gently:

"The truth had to come out, you know."

She sobbed.

"Will they hang him?"

Poirot said:

"A lot has to be proved still. Opportunity — access to poison — the vehicle in which it was administered."

"But supposing, M. Poirot, that he had nothing to do with it — nothing at all?"

"In that case," Poirot shrugged his shoulders, "he will be acquitted."

Nurse Harrison said slowly:

"There is something — something that, I suppose, I ought to have told you before — but I didn't think that there was really anything in it. It was just *queer*."

"I knew there was something," said Poirot. "You had better tell it to me now."

"It isn't much. It's just that one day when I went down to the dispensary for something, Jean Moncrieffe was doing something rather — odd."

"Yes?"

"It sounds so silly. It's only that she was filling up her powder compact — a pink enamel one——"

"Yes?"

"But she wasn't filling it up with powder — with face powder, I mean. She was tipping something into it from one of the bottles out of the poison cupboard. When she saw me she started and shut up the compact and whipped it into her bag — and put back the bottle quickly into the cupboard so that I couldn't see what it was. I daresay it doesn't mean anything — but now I know that Mrs Oldfield really was poisoned——" She broke off.

Poirot said: "You will excuse me?"

He went out and telephoned to Detective Sergeant Grey of the Berkshire Police.

Hercule Poirot came back and he and Nurse Harrison sat in silence.

Poirot was seeing the face of a girl with red hair and hearing a clear hard voice say: "I don't agree." *Jean Moncrieffe had not wanted an autopsy*. She had given a plausible enough excuse, but the fact remained. A competent girl — efficient — resolute. In love with a man who was tied to a complaining invalid wife, who might easily live for years since, according to Nurse Harrison, she had very little the matter with her.

Hercule Poirot sighed.

Nurse Harrison said:

"What are you thinking of?"

Poirot answered:

"The pity of things . . ."

Nurse Harrison said:

"I don't believe for a minute *he* knew anything about it."

Poirot said:

"No. I am sure he did not."

The door opened and Detective Sergeant Grey came in. He had something in his hand, wrapped in a silk handkerchief. He unwrapped it and set it carefully down. It was a bright rose pink enamel compact.

Nurse Harrison said:

"That's the one I saw."

Grey said:

"Found it pushed right to the back of Miss Moncrieffe's bureau drawer. Inside a handkerchief sachet. As far as I can see there are no fingerprints on it, but I'll be careful."

With the handkerchief over his hand he pressed the spring. The case flew open. Grey said:

"This stuff isn't face powder."

He dipped a finger and tasted it gingerly on the tip of his tongue.

"No particular taste."

Poirot said:

"White arsenic does not taste."

Grey said:

"It will be analysed at once." He looked at Nurse Harrison. "You can swear to this being the same case?"

"Yes. I'm positive. That's the case I saw Miss Moncrieffe with in the dispensary about a week before Mrs Oldfield's death."

Sergeant Grey sighed. He looked at Poirot and nodded. The latter rang the bell.

"Send my servant here, please."

George, the perfect valet, discreet, unobtrusive, entered and looked inquiringly at his master.

Hercule Poirot said:

"You have identified this powder compact, Miss Harrison, as one you saw in the possession of Miss Moncrieffe over a year ago. *Would you be surprised to learn that this particular case was sold by Messrs Woolworth only a few weeks ago and that, moreover, it is of a pattern and colour that has only been manufactured for the last three months?*"

Nurse Harrison gasped. She stared at Poirot, her eyes round and dark. Poirot said:

"Have you seen this compact before, Georges?"

George stepped forward:

"Yes, sir. I observed this person, Nurse Harrison, purchase it at Woolworth's on Friday the 18th. Pursuant to your instructions I followed this lady whenever she went out. She took a bus over to Darnington on the day I have mentioned and purchased this compact. She took it home with her. Later, the same day, she came to the house in which Miss Moncrieffe lodges. Acting as by your instructions, I was already in the house. I observed her go into Miss Moncrieffe's bedroom and hide this in the back of the bureau drawer. I had a good view through the crack of the door. She then left the house believing herself unobserved. I may say that no one locks their front doors down here and it was dusk."

Poirot said to Nurse Harrison, and his voice was hard and venomous:

"Can you explain these facts, Nurse Harrison? *I think not*. There was no arsenic in that box when it left Messrs Woolworth, but there was when it left Miss Bristow's house." He added softly, "*It was unwise of you to keep a supply of arsenic in your possession*."

Nurse Harrison buried her face in her hands. She said in a low dull voice:

"*It's true — it's all true . . . I killed her. And all for nothing — nothing . . . I was mad*."

VII

Jean Moncrieffe said:

"I must ask you to forgive me, M. Poirot. I have been so angry with you — so terribly angry with you. It seemed to me that you were making everything so much worse."

Poirot said with a smile:

"So I was to begin with. It is like in the old legend of the Lernean Hydra. Every time a head was cut off, two heads grew in its place. So, to begin with, the rumours grew and multiplied. But you see my task, like that of my namesake Hercules, was to reach the first — the original head. Who had started this rumour? It did not take me long to discover that the originator of the story was Nurse Harrison. I went to see her. She appeared to be a very nice woman — intelligent and sympathetic. But almost at once she made a bad mistake — she repeated to me a conversation which she had overheard taking place between you and the doctor, and that conversation, you see, *was all wrong*. It was psychologically most unlikely. *If* you and the doctor had planned together to kill Mrs Oldfield, you are both of you far too intelligent and level-headed to hold such a conversation in a room with an open door, easily overheard by someone on the stairs or someone in the kitchen. Moreover, the words attributed to you did not fit in at all with your mental make-up. They were the words of a much *older* woman and of one of a quite different type. They were words such as would be imagined by Nurse Harrison as being used *by herself in like circumstances*.

"I had, up to then, regarded the whole matter as fairly simple. Nurse Harrison, I realised, was a fairly young and still-handsome woman — she had been thrown closely with Doctor Oldfield for nearly three years — the doctor had been very fond of her and grateful to her for her tact and sympathy. She had formed the impression that *if Mrs Oldfield died*, the doctor would probably ask her to marry him. Instead of that, after Mrs Oldfield's death, she learns that *Doctor Oldfield is in love with you*. Straightaway, driven by anger and jealousy, she starts spreading the rumour that Doctor Oldfield has poisoned his wife.

"That, as I say, was how I had visualised the position at first. It was a case of a jealous woman and a lying rumour. But the old trite phrase 'no smoke without fire' recurred to me significantly. I wondered if Nurse Harrison had done *more* than spread a rumour. Certain things she said rang strangely. She told me that Mrs Oldfield's illness was largely imaginary — that she did not really suffer much pain. But the *doctor himself* had been in no doubt about the reality of his wife's suffering. *He* had not been surprised by her death. He had called in another doctor shortly before her death and the other doctor had realised the gravity of her condition. Tentatively I brought forward the suggestion of exhumation ... Nurse Harrison was at first frightened out of her wits by the idea. Then, almost at once, her jealousy and hatred took command of her. Let them find arsenic — no suspicion would attach to *her*. It would be the doctor and Jean Moncrieffe who would suffer.

"There was only one hope. *To make Nurse Harrison overreach herself.* If there were a chance that Jean Moncrieffe would escape, I fancied that Nurse Harrison would strain every nerve to involve her in the crime. I gave instructions to my faithful Georges — the most unobtrusive of men whom she did not know by sight. He was to follow her closely. And so — all ended well."

Jean Moncrieffe said:

"You've been *wonderful*."

Dr Oldfield chimed in. He said:

"Yes, indeed. I can never thank you enough. What a blind fool I was!"

Poirot asked curiously:

"Were you as blind, Mademoiselle?"

Jean Moncrieffe said slowly:

"I have been terribly worried. You see, the arsenic in the poison cupboard didn't tally . . ."

Oldfield cried:

"Jean — you didn't think——?"

"No, no — not *you*. What I *did* think was that Mrs Oldfield had somehow or other got hold of it — and that she was taking it so as to make herself ill and get sympathy and that she had inadvertently taken too much. But I was afraid that if there *was* an autopsy and arsenic was found, they would never consider that theory and would leap to the conclusion that *you'd* done it. That's why I never said anything about the missing arsenic. I even cooked the poison book! But the last person I would ever have suspected was Nurse Harrison."

Oldfield said:

"I too. She was such a gentle womanly creature. Like a madonna."

Poirot said sadly:

"Yes, she would have made, probably, a good wife and mother . . . Her emotions were just a little too strong for her." He sighed and murmured once more under his breath:

"*The pity of it.*"

Then he smiled at the happy-looking middle-aged man and the eager-faced girl opposite him. He said to himself:

"These two have come out of its shadow into the sun . . . and I — I have performed the second Labour of Hercules."

The Stymphalian Birds

I

Harold Waring noticed Them first walking up the path from the lake. He was sitting outside the hotel on the terrace. The day was fine, the lake was blue, and the sun shone. Harold was smoking a pipe and feeling that the world was a pretty good place.

His political career was shaping well. An under-secretaryship at the age of thirty was something to be justly proud of. It had been reported that the Prime Minister had said to someone that "young Waring would go far". Harold was, not unnaturally, elated. Life presented itself to him in rosy colours. He was young, sufficiently good-looking, in first-class condition, and quite unencumbered with romantic ties.

He had decided to take a holiday in Herzoslovakia so as to get right off the beaten track and have a real rest from everyone and everything. The hotel at Lake Stempka, though small, was comfortable and not overcrowded. The few people there were mostly foreigners. So far the only other English people were an elderly woman, Mrs Rice, and her married daughter, Mrs Clayton. Harold liked them both. Elsie Clayton was pretty in a rather old-fashioned style. She made up very little, if at all, and was gentle and rather shy. Mrs Rice was what is called a woman of character. She was tall, with a deep voice and a masterful manner, but she had a sense of humour and was good company. Her life was clearly bound up in that of her daughter.

Harold had spent some pleasant hours in the company of mother and daughter, but they did not attempt to monopolise him and relations remained friendly and unexacting between them.

The other people in the hotel had not aroused Harold's notice. Usually they were hikers, or members of a motor-coach tour. They stayed a night or two and then went on. He had hardly noticed anyone else —

until this afternoon.

They came up the path from the lake very slowly and it just happened that at the moment when Harold's attention was attracted to them, a cloud came over the sun. He shivered a little.

Then he stared. Surely there was something odd about these two women? They had long, curved noses, like birds, and their faces, which were curiously alike, were quite immobile. Over their shoulders they wore loose cloaks that flapped in the wind like the wings of two big birds.

Harold thought to himself.

"They *are* like birds." He added almost without volition, "*Birds of ill omen.*"

The women came straight up on the terrace and passed close by him. They were not young — perhaps nearer fifty than forty, and the resemblance between them was so close that they were obviously sisters. Their expression was forbidding. As they passed Harold the eyes of both of them rested on him for a minute. It was a curious, appraising glance — almost inhuman.

Harold's impression of evil grew stronger. He noticed the hand of one of the two sisters, a long claw-like hand . . .

Although the sun had come out, he shivered once again. He thought: "Horrible creatures. Like birds of prey . . ."

He was distracted from these imaginings by the emergence of Mrs Rice from the hotel. He jumped up and drew forward a chair. With a word of thanks she sat down and, as usual, began to knit vigorously.

Harold asked:

"Did you see those two women who just went into the hotel?"

"With cloaks on? Yes, I passed them."

"Extraordinary creatures, didn't you think?"

"Well — yes, perhaps they are rather odd. They only arrived yesterday, I think. Very alike — they must be twins."

Harold said:

"I may be fanciful, but I distinctly felt there was something evil about them."

"How curious. I must look at them more closely and see if I agree with you."

She added: "We'll find out from the *concierge* who they are. Not English, I imagine?"

"Oh no."

Mrs Rice glanced at her watch. She said:

"Teatime. I wonder if you'd mind going in and ringing the bell, Mr Waring?"

"Certainly, Mrs Rice."

He did so and then as he returned to his seat he asked:

"Where's your daughter this afternoon?"

"Elsie? We went for a walk together. Part of the way round the lake and then back through the pinewoods. It really was lovely."

A waiter came out and received orders for tea. Mrs Rice went on, her needles flying vigorously:

"Elsie had a letter from her husband. She mayn't come down to tea."

"Her husband?" Harold was surprised. "Do you know, I always thought she was a widow."

Mrs Rice shot him a sharp glance. She said dryly:

"Oh no, Elsie isn't a widow." She added with emphasis: "Unfortunately!"

Harold was startled.

Mrs Rice, nodding her head grimly, said:

"Drink is responsible for a lot of unhappiness, Mr Waring."

"Does he drink?"

"Yes. And a good many other things as well. He's insanely jealous and has a singularly violent temper." She sighed. "It's a difficult world, Mr Waring. I'm devoted to Elsie, she's my only child — and to see her unhappy isn't an easy thing to bear."

Harold said with real emotion:

"She's such a gentle creature."

"A little too gentle, perhaps."

"You mean——"

Mrs Rice said slowly:

"A happy creature is more arrogant. Elsie's gentleness comes, I think, from a sense of defeat. Life has been too much for her."

Harold said with some slight hesitation:

"How — did she come to marry this husband of hers?"

Mrs Rice answered:

"Philip Clayton was a very attractive person. He had — still has — great charm, he had a certain amount of money — and there was no one to advise us of his real character. I had been a widow for many years. Two women, living alone, are not the best judges of a man's character."

Harold said thoughtfully:

"No, that's true."

He felt a wave of indignation and pity sweep over him. Elsie Clayton could not be more than twenty-five at the most. He recalled the clear friendliness of her blue eyes, the soft droop of her mouth. He realised, suddenly, that his interest in her went a little beyond friendship.

And she was tied to a brute . . .

II

That evening, Harold joined mother and daughter after dinner. Elsie Clayton was wearing a soft dull pink dress. Her eyelids, he noticed, were red. She had been crying.

Mrs Rice said briskly:

"I've found out who your two harpies are, Mr Waring. Polish ladies — of very good family, so the *concierge* says."

Harold looked across the room to where the Polish ladies were sitting.

Elsie said with interest:

"Those two women over there? With the henna-dyed hair? They look rather horrible somehow — I don't know why."

Harold said triumphantly:

"That's just what I thought."

Mrs Rice said with a laugh:

"I think you are both being absurd. You can't possibly tell what people are like just by looking at them."

Elsie laughed.

She said:

"I suppose one can't. All the same *I* think they're vultures!"

"Picking out dead men's eyes!" said Harold.

"Oh, don't," cried Elsie.

Harold said quickly:

"Sorry."

Mrs Rice said with a smile:

"Anyway they're not likely to cross *our* path."

Elsie said:

"*We* haven't got any guilty secrets!"

"Perhaps Mr Waring has," said Mrs Rice with a twinkle.

Harold laughed, throwing his head back.

He said:

"Not a secret in the world. My life's an open book."

And it flashed across his mind:

"What fools people are who leave the straight path. A clear conscience — that's all one needs in life. With that you can face the world and tell everyone who interferes with you to go to the devil!"

He felt suddenly very much alive — very strong — very much master of his fate!

III

Harold Waring, like many other Englishmen, was a bad linguist. His French was halting and decidedly British in intonation. Of German and Italian he knew nothing.

Up to now, these linguistic disabilities had not worried him. In most hotels on the Continent, he had always found, everyone spoke English, so why worry?

But in this out-of-the-way spot, where the native language was a form of Slovak and even the *concierge* only spoke German it was sometimes galling to Harold when one of his two women friends acted as interpreter for him. Mrs Rice, who was fond of languages, could even speak a little Slovak.

Harold determined that he would set about learning German. He decided to buy some textbooks and spend a couple of hours each morning in mastering the language.

The morning was fine and, after writing some letters, Harold looked at his watch and saw there was still time for an hour's stroll before lunch. He went down towards the lake and then turned aside into the pinewoods. He had walked there for perhaps five minutes when he heard an unmistakable sound. Somewhere not far away a woman was sobbing her heart out.

Harold paused a minute, then he went in the direction of the sound. The woman was Elsie Clayton and she was sitting on a fallen tree with her face buried in her hands and her shoulders quivering with the violence of her grief.

Harold hesitated a minute, then he came up to her. He said gently:

"Mrs Clayton — Elsie?"

She started violently and looked up at him. Harold sat down beside her.

He said with real sympathy:

"Is there anything I can do? Anything at all?"

She shook her head.

"No — no — you're very kind. But there's nothing that anyone can do for me."

Harold said rather diffidently:

"Is it to do with — your husband?"

She nodded. Then she wiped her eyes and took out her powder compact, struggling to regain command of herself. She said in a quavering voice:

"I didn't want Mother to worry. She's so upset when she sees me unhappy. So I came out here to have a good cry. It's silly, I know. Crying doesn't help. But — sometimes — one just feels that life is quite unbearable."

Harold said:

"I'm terribly sorry."

She threw him a grateful glance. Then she said hurriedly:

"It's my own fault, of course. I married Philip of my own free will. It — it's turned out badly, I've only myself to blame."

Harold said:

"It's very plucky of you to put it like that."

Elsie shook her head.

"No, I'm not plucky. I'm not brave at all. I'm an awful coward. That's partly the trouble with Philip. I'm terrified of him — absolutely terrified — when he gets in one of his rages."

Harold said with feeling:

"You ought to leave him!"

"I daren't. He — he wouldn't let me."

"Nonsense! What about a divorce?"

She shook her head slowly.

"I've no grounds." She straightened her shoulders. "No, I've got to carry on. I spend a fair amount of time with Mother, you know. Philip doesn't mind that. Especially when we go somewhere off the beaten track like this." She added, the colour rising in her cheeks, "You see, part of the trouble is that he's insanely jealous. If — if I so much as speak to another man he makes the most frightful scenes."

Harold's indignation rose. He had heard many women complain of the jealousy of a husband, and whilst professing sympathy, had been secretly of the opinion that the husband was amply justified. But Elsie Clayton was not one of those women. She had never thrown him so much as a flirtatious glance.

Elsie drew away from him with a slight shiver. She glanced up at the sky.

"The sun's gone in. It's quite cold. We'd better get back to the hotel. It must be nearly lunchtime."

They got up and turned in the direction of the hotel. They had walked for perhaps a minute when they overtook a figure going in the same direction. They recognised her by the flapping cloak she wore. It was one of the Polish sisters.

They passed her, Harold bowing slightly. She made no response, but her eyes rested on them both for a minute and there was a certain appraising quality in the glance which made Harold feel suddenly hot. He wondered if the woman had seen him sitting by Elsie on the tree trunk. If so, she probably thought . . .

Well, she looked as though she thought . . . A wave of indignation overwhelmed him! What foul minds some women had!

Odd that the sun had gone in and that they should both have shivered — perhaps just at the moment that that woman was watching them . . .

Somehow, Harold felt a little uneasy.

IV

That evening, Harold went to his room a little after ten. The English mail had arrived and he had received a number of letters, some of which needed immediate answers.

He got into his pyjamas and a dressing gown and sat down at the desk to deal with his correspondence. He had written three letters and was just starting on the fourth when the door was suddenly flung open and Elsie Clayton staggered into the room.

Harold jumped up, startled. Elsie had pushed the door to behind her and was standing clutching at the chest of drawers. Her breath was coming in great gasps, her face was the colour of chalk. She looked frightened to death.

She gasped out: "It's my husband! He arrived unexpectedly. I — I think he'll kill me. He's mad — quite mad. I came to you. Don't — don't let him find me."

She took a step or two forward, swaying so much that she almost fell. Harold put out an arm to support her.

As he did so, the door was flung open and a man stood in the doorway. He was of medium height with thick eyebrows and a sleek, dark head. In his hand he carried a heavy car spanner. His voice rose high and shook with rage. He almost screamed the words.

"So that Polish woman was right! You *are* carrying on with this fellow!"

Elsie cried:

"No, no, Philip. It's not true. You're wrong."

Harold thrust the girl swiftly behind him, as Philip Clayton advanced on them both. The latter cried:

"Wrong, am I? When I find you here in his room? You she-devil, I'll kill you for this."

With a swift, sideways movement he dodged Harold's arm. Elsie, with a cry, ran round the other side of Harold, who swung round to fend the other off.

But Philip Clayton had only one idea, to get at his wife. He swerved round again. Elsie, terrified, rushed out of the room. Philip Clayton dashed after her, and Harold, with not a moment's hesitation, followed him.

Elsie had darted back into her own bedroom at the end of the corridor. Harold could hear the sound of the key turning in the lock, but it did not turn in time. Before the lock could catch, Philip Clayton wrenched the door open. He disappeared into the room and Harold heard Elsie's frightened cry.

In another minute Harold burst in after them.

Elsie was standing at bay against the curtains of the window. As Harold entered Philip Clayton rushed at her brandishing the spanner. She gave a terrified cry, then snatching up a heavy paperweight from the desk beside her, she flung it at him.

Clayton went down like a log. Elsie screamed. Harold stopped petrified in the doorway. The girl fell on her knees beside her husband. He lay quite still where he had fallen.

Outside in the passage, there was the sound of the bolt of one of the doors being drawn back. Elsie jumped up and ran to Harold.

"Please — please——" Her voice was low and breathless. "Go back to your room. They'll come — they'll find you here."

Harold nodded. He took in the situation like lightning. For the moment, Philip Clayton was *hors de combat*. But Elsie's scream might have been heard. If he were found in her room it could only cause embarrassment and misunderstanding. Both for her sake and his own there must be no scandal.

As noiselessly as possible, he sprinted down the passage and back into his room. Just as he reached it, he heard the sound of an opening door.

He sat in his room for nearly half an hour, waiting. He dared not go out. Sooner or later, he felt sure, Elsie would come.

There was a light tap on his door. Harold jumped up to open it.

It was not Elsie who came in, but her mother, and Harold was aghast at her appearance. She looked suddenly years older. Her grey hair was dishevelled and there were deep black circles under her eyes.

He sprang up and helped her to a chair. She sat down, her breath coming painfully. Harold said quickly:

"You look all in, Mrs Rice. Can I get you something?"

She shook her head.

"No. Never mind me. I'm all right, really. It's only the shock. Mr Waring, a terrible thing has happened."

Harold asked:

"Is Clayton seriously injured?"

She caught her breath.

"Worse than that. *He's dead* . . ."

V

The room spun round.

A feeling as of icy water trickling down his spine rendered Harold incapable of speech for a moment or two.

He repeated dully:

"*Dead?*"

Mrs Rice nodded.

She said, and her voice had the flat level tones of complete exhaustion:

"The corner of that marble paperweight caught him right on the temple and he fell back with his head on the iron fender. I don't know which it was that killed him — but he is certainly dead. I have seen death often enough to know."

Disaster — that was the word that rang insistently in Harold's brain. Disaster, disaster, disaster . . .

He said vehemently:

"It was an accident . . . I saw it happen."

Mrs Rice said sharply:

"Of course it was an accident. *I* know that. But — but — is anyone else going to think so? I'm — frankly, I'm frightened, Harold! This isn't England."

Harold said slowly:

"I can confirm Elsie's story."

Mrs Rice said:

"Yes, and she can confirm yours. That — that is just it!"

Harold's brain, naturally a keen and cautious one, saw her point. He reviewed the whole thing and appreciated the weakness of their position.

He and Elsie had spent a good deal of their time together. Then there was the fact that they had been seen together in the pinewoods by one of the Polish women under rather compromising circumstances. The Polish ladies apparently spoke no English, but they might nevertheless understand it a little. The woman might have known the meaning of words like "jealousy" and "husband" if she had chanced to overhear their conversation. Anyway it was clear that it was something she had said to Clayton that had aroused his jealousy. And now — his death. When Clayton had died, he, Harold, *had been in Elsie Clayton's room*. There was nothing to show that he had not deliberately assaulted Philip Clayton with the paperweight. Nothing to show that the jealous husband had not actually found them together. There was only his word and Elsie's. Would they be believed?

A cold fear gripped him.

He did not imagine — *no*, he really did *not* imagine — that either he or Elsie was in danger of being condemned to death for a murder they had not committed. Surely, in any case, it could be only a charge of manslaughter brought against them. (Did they have manslaughter in these foreign countries?) But even if they were acquitted of blame there would have to be an inquiry — it would be reported in all the papers. *An English man and woman accused — jealous husband — rising politician.* Yes, it would mean the end of his political career. It would never survive a scandal like that.

He said on an impulse:

"Can't we get rid of the body somehow? Plant it somewhere?"

Mrs Rice's astonished and scornful look made him blush. She said incisively:

"My dear Harold, this isn't a detective story! To attempt a thing like that would be quite crazy."

"I suppose it would." He groaned. "What can we do? My God, what can we do?"

Mrs Rice shook her head despairingly. She was frowning, her mind working painfully.

Harold demanded:

"Isn't there anything we can do? Anything to avoid this frightful disaster?"

There, it was out — disaster! Terrible — unforeseen — utterly damning.

They stared at each other. Mrs Rice said hoarsely:

"Elsie — my little girl. I'd do anything . . . It will kill her if she has to go through a thing like this." And she added: "You too, your career — everything."

Harold managed to say:

"Never mind me."

But he did not really mean it.

Mrs Rice went on bitterly:

"And all so unfair — so utterly untrue! It's not as though there had ever been anything between you. I know that well enough."

Harold suggested, catching at a straw:

"You'll be able to say that at least — that it was all perfectly all right."

Mrs Rice said bitterly:

"Yes, if they believe me. But you know what these people out here are like!"

Harold agreed gloomily. To the Continental mind, there would undoubtedly be a guilty connection between himself and Elsie, and all Mrs Rice's denials would be taken as a mother lying herself black in the face for her daughter.

Harold said gloomily:

"Yes, we're not in England, worse luck."

"Ah!" Mrs Rice lifted her head. "*That's* true . . . It's not England. I wonder now if something *could* be done——"

"Yes?" Harold looked at her eagerly.

Mrs Rice said abruptly:

"How much money have you got?"

"Not much with me." He added: "I could wire for money, of course."

Mrs Rice said grimly: "We may need a good deal. But I think it's worth trying."

Harold felt a faint lifting of despair. He said:

"What is your idea?"

Mrs Rice spoke decisively.

"We haven't a chance of concealing the death *ourselves,* but I do think there's just a chance of hushing it up *officially*!"

"You really think so?" Harold was hopeful but slightly incredulous.

"Yes, for one thing the manager of the hotel will be on our side. He'd much rather have the thing hushed up. It's my opinion that in these out-of-the-way curious little Balkan countries you can bribe anyone and everyone — and the police are probably more corrupt than anyone else!"

Harold said slowly:

"Do you know, I believe you're right."

Mrs Rice went on:

"Fortunately, I don't think anyone in the hotel *heard* anything."

"Who has the room next to Elsie's on the other side from yours?"

"The two Polish ladies. They didn't hear anything. They'd have come out into the passage if they had. Philip arrived late, nobody saw him but the night porter. Do you know, Harold, I believe it will be possible to hush the whole thing up — and get Philip's death certified as due to natural causes! It's just a question of bribing high enough — and finding the right man — probably the Chief of Police!"

Harold smiled faintly. He said:

"It's rather Comic Opera, isn't it? Well, after all, we can but try."

VI

Mrs Rice was energy personified. First the manager was summoned. Harold remained in his room, keeping out of it. He and Mrs Rice had agreed that the story told had better be that of a quarrel between husband and wife. Elsie's youth and prettiness would command more sympathy.

On the following morning various police officials arrived and were shown up to Mrs Rice's bedroom. They left at midday. Harold had wired for money but otherwise had taken no part in the proceedings — indeed he would have been unable to do so since none of these official personages spoke English.

At twelve o'clock Mrs Rice came to his room. She looked white and tired, but the relief on her face told its own story. She said simply:

"It's *worked*!"

"Thank heaven! You've really been marvellous! It seems incredible!"

Mrs Rice said thoughtfully:

"By the ease with which it went, you might almost think it was quite normal. They practically held out their hands right away. It's — it's rather disgusting, really!"

Harold said dryly:

"This isn't the moment to quarrel with the corruption of the public services. How much?"

"The tariff's rather high."

She read out a list of figures.

"The Chief of Police.

The *Commissaire*.

The *Agent*.

The Doctor.

The Hotel Manager.

The Night Porter."

Harold's comment was merely:

"The night porter doesn't get much, does he? I suppose it's mostly a question of gold lace."

Mrs Rice explained:

"The manager stipulated that the death should not have taken place in his hotel at all. The official story will be that Philip had a heart attack in the train. He went along the corridor for air — you know how they always leave those doors open — and he fell out on the line. It's wonderful what the police can do when they try!"

"Well," said Harold. "Thank God *our* police force isn't like that."

And in a British and superior mood he went down to lunch.

VII

After lunch Harold usually joined Mrs Rice and her daughter for coffee. He decided to make no change in his usual behaviour.

This was the first time he had seen Elsie since the night before. She was very pale and was obviously still suffering from shock, but she made a gallant endeavour to behave as usual, uttering small commonplaces about the weather and the scenery.

They commented on a new guest who had just arrived, trying to guess his nationality. Harold thought a moustache like that must be French — Elsie said German — and Mrs Rice thought he might be Spanish.

There was no one else but themselves on the terrace with the exception of the two Polish ladies who were sitting at the extreme end, both doing fancywork.

As always when he saw them, Harold felt a queer shiver of apprehension pass over him. Those still faces, those curved beaks of noses, those long claw-like hands . . .

A pageboy approached and told Mrs Rice she was wanted. She rose and followed him. At the entrance to the hotel they saw her encounter a police official in full uniform.

Elsie caught her breath.

"You don't think — anything's gone wrong?"

Harold reassured her quickly.

"Oh no, no, nothing of that kind."

But he himself knew a sudden pang of fear.

He said:

"Your mother's been wonderful!"

"I know. Mother is a great fighter. She'll never sit down under defeat." Elsie shivered. "But it is all horrible, isn't it?"

"Now, don't dwell on it. It's all over and done with."

Elsie said in a low voice:

"I can't forget that — that it was *I* who killed him."

Harold said urgently:

"Don't think of it that way. It was an accident. You know that really."

Her face grew a little happier. Harold added:

"And anyway it's past. The past is the past. Try never to think of it again."

Mrs Rice came back. By the expression on her face they saw that all was well.

"It gave me quite a fright," she said almost gaily. "But it was only a formality about some papers. Everything's all right, my children. We're out of the shadow. I think we might order ourselves a liqueur on the strength of it."

The liqueur was ordered and came. They raised their glasses.

Mrs Rice said: "To the Future!"

Harold smiled at Elsie and said:

"To your happiness!"

She smiled back at him and said as she lifted her glass:

"And to you — to your success! I'm sure you're going to be a very great man."

With the reaction from fear they felt gay, almost light-headed. The shadow had lifted! All was well . . .

From the far end of the terrace the two bird-like women rose. They rolled up their work carefully. They came across the stone flags.

With little bows they sat down by Mrs Rice. One of them began to speak. The other one let her eyes rest on Elsie and Harold. There was a little smile on her lips. It was not, Harold thought, a nice smile . . .

He looked over at Mrs Rice. She was listening to the Polish woman and though he couldn't understand a word, the expression on Mrs Rice's face was clear enough. All the old anguish and despair came back. She listened and occasionally spoke a brief word.

Presently the two sisters rose, and with stiff little bows went into the hotel.

Harold leaned forward. He said hoarsely:

"What is it?"

Mrs Rice answered him in the quiet hopeless tones of despair.

"Those women are going to blackmail us. They heard everything last night. And now we've tried to hush it up, it makes the whole thing a thousand times worse . . ."

VIII

Harold Waring was down by the lake. He had been walking feverishly for over an hour, trying by sheer physical energy to still the clamour of despair that had attacked him.

He came at last to the spot where he had first noticed the two grim women who held his life and Elsie's in their evil talons. He said aloud:

"Curse them! Damn them for a pair of devilish bloodsucking harpies!"

A slight cough made him spin round. He found himself facing the luxuriantly moustached stranger who had just come out from the shade of the trees.

Harold found it difficult to know what to say. This little man must have almost certainly overheard what he had just said.

Harold, at a loss, said somewhat ridiculously:

"Oh — er — good afternoon."

In perfect English the other replied:

"But for you, I fear, it is not a good afternoon?"

"Well — er — I——" Harold was in difficulties again.

The little man said:

"You are, I think, in trouble, Monsieur? Can I be of any assistance to you?"

"Oh no thanks, no thanks! Just blowing off steam, you know."

The other said gently:

"But I think, you know, that I *could* help you. I am correct, am I not, in connecting your troubles with two ladies who were sitting on the terrace just now?"

Harold stared at him.

"Do you know anything about them?" He added: "Who are you, anyway?"

As though confessing to royal birth the little man said modestly:

"*I am Hercule Poirot.* Shall we walk a little way into the wood and you shall tell me your story? As I say, I think I can aid you."

To this day, Harold is not quite certain what made him suddenly pour out the whole story to a man to whom he had only spoken a few minutes before. Perhaps it was overstrain. Anyway, it happened. He told Hercule

Poirot the whole story.

The latter listened in silence. Once or twice he nodded his head gravely. When Harold came to a stop the other spoke dreamily.

"The Stymphalian Birds, with iron beaks, who feed on human flesh and who dwell by the Stymphalian Lake . . . Yes, it accords very well."

"I beg your pardon," said Harold staring.

Perhaps, he thought, this curious-looking little man was mad!

Hercule Poirot smiled.

"I reflect, that is all. I have my own way of looking at things, you understand. Now as to this business of yours. You are very unpleasantly placed."

Harold said impatiently:

"I don't need you to tell me that!"

Hercule Poirot went on:

"It is a serious business, blackmail. These harpies will force you to pay — and pay — and pay again! And if you defy them, well, what happens?"

Harold said bitterly:

"The whole thing comes out. My career's ruined, and a wretched girl who's never done anyone any harm will be put through hell, and God knows what the end of it all will be!"

"Therefore," said Hercule Poirot, "something must be done!"

Harold said baldly: "What?"

Hercule Poirot leaned back, half-closing his eyes. He said (and again a doubt of his sanity crossed Harold's mind):

"It is the moment for the castanets of bronze."

Harold said:

"Are you quite mad?"

The other shook his head. He said:

"*Mais non!* I strive only to follow the example of my great predecessor, Hercules. Have a few hours' patience, my friend. By tomorrow I may be able to deliver you from your persecutors."

IX

Harold Waring came down the following morning to find Hercule Poirot sitting alone on the terrace. In spite of himself Harold had been impressed by Hercule Poirot's promises.

He came up to him now and asked anxiously:

"Well?"

Hercule Poirot beamed upon him.

"It is well."

"What do you mean?"

"Everything has settled itself satisfactorily."

"But what has *happened*?"

Hercule Poirot replied dreamily:

"I have employed the castanets of bronze. Or, in modern parlance, I have caused metal wires to hum — in short I have employed the telegraph! Your Stymphalian Birds, Monsieur, have been removed to where they will be unable to exercise their ingenuity for some time to come."

"They were wanted by the police. They have been arrested?"

"Precisely."

Harold drew a deep breath.

"How marvellous! I never thought of that." He got up. "I must find Mrs Rice and Elsie and tell them."

"They know."

"Oh good." Harold sat down again. "Tell me just what——"

He broke off.

Coming up the path from the lake were two figures with flapping cloaks and profiles like birds.

He exclaimed:

"I thought you said they had been taken away!"

Hercule Poirot followed his glance.

"Oh, those ladies? They are very harmless; Polish ladies of good family, as the porter told you. Their appearance is, perhaps, not very pleasing, but that is all."

"But I don't *understand*!"

"No, you do not understand! It is the *other* ladies who were wanted by the police — the resourceful Mrs Rice and her lachrymose Mrs Clayton! It is *they* who are well-known birds of prey. Those two, they make their living by blackmail, *mon cher*."

Harold had a sensation of the world spinning round him. He said faintly:

"But the man — the man who was killed?"

"No one was killed. There was no man!"

"But I *saw* him!"

"Oh no. The tall deep-voiced Mrs Rice is a very successful male impersonator. It was she who played the part of the husband — without her grey wig and suitably made up for the part."

He leaned forward and tapped the other on the knee.

"You must not go through life being too credulous, my friend. The police of a country are not so easily bribed — they are probably not to be bribed at all — certainly not when it is a question of murder! These women trade on the average Englishman's ignorance of foreign languages. Because she speaks French or German, it is always this Mrs Rice who interviews the manager and takes charge of the affair. The police arrive and go to *her* room, yes! But what actually passes? *You* do not know. Perhaps she says she has lost a brooch — something of that kind. Any excuse to arrange for the police to come *so that you shall see them*. For the rest, what actually happens? You wire for money, a lot of money, and you hand it over to Mrs Rice who is in charge of all the negotiations! And that is that! But they are greedy, these birds of prey. They have seen that you have taken an unreasonable aversion to these two unfortunate Polish ladies. The ladies in question come and hold a perfectly innocent conversation with Mrs Rice and she cannot resist repeating the game. She knows you cannot understand what is being said.

"So you will have to send for more money which Mrs Rice will pretend to distribute to a fresh set of people."

Harold drew a deep breath. He said:

"And Elsie — Elsie?"

Hercule Poirot averted his eyes.

"She played her part very well. She always does. A most accomplished little actress. Everything is very pure — very innocent. She appeals, not to sex, but to chivalry."

Hercule Poirot added dreamily:

"That is always successful with Englishmen."

Harold Waring drew a deep breath. He said crisply:

"I'm going to set to work and learn every European language there is! Nobody's going to make a fool of me a second time!"

Tape-Measure Murder

Miss Politt took hold of the knocker and rapped politely on the cottage door. After a discreet interval she knocked again. The parcel under her left arm shifted a little as she did so, and she readjusted it. Inside the parcel was Mrs Spenlow's new green winter dress, ready for fitting. From Miss Politt's left hand dangled a bag of black silk, containing a tape measure, a pincushion, and a large, practical pair of scissors.

Miss Politt was tall and gaunt, with a sharp nose, pursed lips, and meagre iron-grey hair. She hesitated before using the knocker for the third time. Glancing down the street, she saw a figure rapidly approaching. Miss Hartnell, jolly, weather-beaten, fifty-five, shouted out in her usual loud bass voice, "Good afternoon, Miss Politt!"

The dressmaker answered, "Good afternoon, Miss Hartnell." Her voice was excessively thin and genteel in its accents. She had started life as a lady's maid. "Excuse me," she went on, "but do you happen to know if by any chance Mrs Spenlow isn't at home?"

"Not the least idea," said Miss Hartnell.

"It's rather awkward, you see. I was to fit on Mrs Spenlow's new dress this afternoon. Three thirty, she said."

Miss Hartnell consulted her wristwatch. "It's a little past the half-hour now."

"Yes. I have knocked three times, but there doesn't seem to be any answer, so I was wondering if perhaps Mrs Spenlow might have gone out and forgotten. She doesn't forget appointments as a rule, and she wants the dress to wear the day after tomorrow."

Miss Hartnell entered the gate and walked up the path to join Miss Politt outside the door of Laburnum Cottage.

"Why doesn't Gladys answer the door?" she demanded. "Oh, no, of course, it's Thursday — Gladys's day out. I expect Mrs Spenlow has fallen asleep. I don't expect you've made enough noise with this thing."

Seizing the knocker, she executed a deafening *rat-a-tat-tat*, and in addition thumped upon the panels of the door. She also called out in a stentorian voice, "What ho, within there!"

There was no response.

Miss Politt murmured, "Oh, I think Mrs Spenlow must have forgotten and gone out. I'll call round some other time." She began edging away down the path.

"Nonsense," said Miss Hartnell firmly. "She can't have gone out. I'd have met her. I'll just take a look through the windows and see if I can find any signs of life."

She laughed in her usual hearty manner, to indicate that it was a joke, and applied a perfunctory glance to the nearest windowpane — perfunctory because she knew quite well that the front room was seldom used, Mr and Mrs Spenlow preferring the small back sitting room.

Perfunctory as it was, though, it succeeded in its object. Miss Hartnell, it is true, saw no signs of life. On the contrary, she saw, through the window, Mrs Spenlow lying on the hearthrug — dead.

"Of course," said Miss Hartnell, telling the story afterwards, "I managed to keep my head. That Politt creature wouldn't have had the least idea of what to do. 'Got to keep our heads,' I said to her. '*You* stay here, and I'll go for Constable Palk.' She said something about not wanting to be left, but I paid no attention at all. One has to be firm with that sort of person. I've always found they enjoy making a fuss. So I was just going off when, at that very moment, Mr Spenlow came round the corner of the house."

Here Miss Hartnell made a significant pause. It enabled her audience to ask breathlessly, "Tell me, how did he *look*?"

Miss Hartnell would then go on, "Frankly, *I* suspected something at once! He was *far* too calm. He didn't seem surprised in the least. And you may say what you like, it isn't natural for a man to hear that his wife is dead and display no emotion whatever."

Everybody agreed with this statement.

The police agreed with it, too. So suspicious did they consider Mr Spenlow's detachment, that they lost no time in ascertaining how that gentleman was situated as a result of his wife's death. When they discovered that Mrs Spenlow had been the monied partner, and that her money went to her husband under a will made soon after their marriage, they were more suspicious than ever.

Miss Marple, that sweet-faced — and, some said, vinegar-tongued — elderly spinster who lived in the house next to the rectory, was interviewed very early — within half an hour of the discovery of the crime. She was approached by Police Constable Palk, importantly thumbing a notebook. "If you don't mind, ma'am, I've a few questions to ask you."

Miss Marple said, "In connection with the murder of Mrs Spenlow?"

Palk was startled. "May I ask, madam, how you got to know of it?"

"The fish," said Miss Marple.

The reply was perfectly intelligible to Constable Palk. He assumed correctly that the fishmonger's boy had brought it, together with Miss Marple's evening meal.

Miss Marple continued gently. "Lying on the floor in the sitting room, strangled — possibly by a very narrow belt. But whatever it was, it was taken away."

Palk's face was wrathful. "How that young Fred gets to know everything——"

Miss Marple cut him short adroitly. She said, "There's a pin in your tunic."

Constable Palk looked down, startled. He said, "They do say, 'See a pin and pick it up, all the day you'll have good luck.'"

"I hope that will come true. Now what is it you want me to tell you?"

Constable Palk cleared his throat, looked important, and consulted his notebook. "Statement was made to me by Mr Arthur Spenlow, husband of the deceased. Mr Spenlow says that at two thirty, as far as he can say, he was rung up by Miss Marple, and asked if he would come over at a quarter past three as she was anxious to consult him about something. Now, ma'am, is that true?"

"Certainly not," said Miss Marple.

"You did not ring up Mr Spenlow at two thirty!"

"Neither at two thirty nor any other time."

"Ah," said Constable Palk, and sucked his moustache with a good deal of satisfaction.

"What else did Mr Spenlow say?"

"Mr Spenlow's statement was that he came over here as requested, leaving his own house at ten minutes past three; that on arrival here he was informed by the maid servant that Miss Marple was 'not at 'ome'."

"That part of it is true," said Miss Marple. "He did come here, but I was at a meeting at the Women's Institute."

"Ah," said Constable Palk again.

Miss Marple exclaimed, "Do tell me, Constable, do you suspect Mr Spenlow?"

"It's not for me to say at this stage, but it looks to me as though somebody, naming no names, had been trying to be artful."

Miss Marple said thoughtfully, "Mr Spenlow?"

She liked Mr Spenlow. He was a small, spare man, stiff and conventional in speech, the acme of respectability. It seemed odd that he should have come to live in the country, he had so clearly lived in towns all his life. To Miss Marple he confided the reason. He said, "I have always intended, ever since I was a small boy, to live in the country some day and have a garden of my own. I have always been very much attached to flowers. My wife, you know, kept a flower shop. That's where I saw her first."

A dry statement, but it opened up a vista of romance. A younger, prettier Mrs Spenlow, seen against a background of flowers.

Mr Spenlow, however, really knew nothing about flowers. He had no idea of seeds, of cuttings, of bedding out, of annuals or perennials. He had only a vision — a vision of a small cottage garden thickly planted with sweet-smelling, brightly coloured blossoms. He had asked, almost pathetically, for instruction, and had noted down Miss Marple's replies to questions in a little book.

He was a man of quiet method. It was, perhaps, because of this trait, that the police were interested in him when his wife was found murdered. With patience and perseverance they learned a good deal about the late Mrs Spenlow — and soon all St Mary Mead knew it, too.

The late Mrs Spenlow had begun life as a between-maid in a large house. She had left that position to marry the second gardener, and with him had started a flower shop in London. The shop had prospered. Not so the gardener, who before long had sickened and died.

His widow carried on the shop and enlarged it in an ambitious way. She had continued to prosper. Then she had sold the business at a handsome price and embarked upon matrimony for the second time — with Mr Spenlow, a middle-aged jeweller who had inherited a small and struggling business. Not long afterwards, they had sold the business and come down to St Mary Mead.

Mrs Spenlow was a well-to-do woman. The profits from her florist's establishment she had invested — "under spirit guidance", as she explained to all and sundry. The spirits had advised her with unexpected acumen.

All her investments had prospered, some in quite a sensational fashion. Instead, however, of this increasing her belief in spiritualism, Mrs Spenlow basely deserted mediums and sittings, and made a brief but wholehearted plunge into an obscure religion with Indian affinities which was based on various forms of deep breathing. When, however, she arrived at St Mary Mead, she had relapsed into a period of orthodox Church-of-England beliefs. She was a good deal at the vicarage, and attended church services with assiduity. She patronised the village shops, took an interest in the local happenings, and played village bridge.

A humdrum, everyday life. And — suddenly — murder.

Colonel Melchett, the chief constable, had summoned Inspector Slack.

Slack was a positive type of man. When he had made up his mind, he was sure. He was quite sure now. "Husband did it, sir," he said.

"You think so?"

"Quite sure of it. You've only got to look at him. Guilty as hell. Never showed a sign of grief or emotion. He came back to the house knowing she was dead."

"Wouldn't he at least have tried to act the part of the distracted husband?"

"Not him, sir. Too pleased with himself. Some gentlemen can't act. Too stiff."

"Any other woman in his life?" Colonel Melchett asked.

"Haven't been able to find any trace of one. Of course, he's the artful kind. He'd cover his tracks. As I see it, he was just fed up with his wife. She'd got the money, and I should say was a trying woman to live with — always taking up with some 'ism' or other. He cold-bloodedly decided to do away with her and live comfortably on his own."

"Yes, that could be the case, I suppose."

"Depend upon it, that was it. Made his plans careful. Pretended to get a phone call——"

Melchett interrupted him. "No call been traced?"

"No, sir. That means either that he lied, or that the call was put through from a public telephone booth. The only two public phones in the village are at the station and the post office. Post office it certainly wasn't. Mrs Blade sees everyone who comes in. Station it might be. Train arrives at two twenty-seven and there's a bit of a bustle then. But the main thing is *he* says it was Miss Marple who called him up, and that certainly isn't true. The call didn't come from her house, and she herself was away at the Institute."

"You're not overlooking the possibility that the husband was deliberately got out of the way — by someone who wanted to murder Mrs Spenlow?"

"You're thinking of young Ted Gerard, aren't you, sir? I've been working on him — what we're up against there is lack of motive. He doesn't stand to gain anything."

"He's an undesirable character, though. Quite a pretty little spot of embezzlement to his credit."

"I'm not saying he isn't a wrong 'un. Still, he did go to his boss and own up to that embezzlement. And his employers weren't wise to it."

"An Oxford Grouper,"* said Melchett.

"Yes, sir. Became a convert and went off to do the straight thing and own up to having pinched money. I'm not saying, mind you, that it mayn't have been astuteness. He may have thought he was suspected and decided to gamble on honest repentance."

"You have a sceptical mind, Slack," said Colonel Melchett. "By the way, have you talked to Miss Marple at all?"

"What's *she* got to do with it, sir?"

"Oh, nothing. But she hears things, you know. Why don't you go and have a chat with her? She's a very sharp old lady."

Slack changed the subject. "One thing I've been meaning to ask you, sir. That domestic-service job where the deceased started her career — Sir Robert Abercrombie's place. That's where that jewel robbery was — emeralds — worth a packet. Never got them. I've been looking it up

---

*Oxford Group: a religious movement, whose members publicly confessed their faults

— must have happened when the Spenlow woman was there, though she'd have been quite a girl at the time. Don't think she was mixed up in it, do you, sir? Spenlow, you know, was one of those little tuppenny-ha'penny jewellers — just the chap for a fence."

Melchett shook his head. "Don't think there's anything in that. She didn't even know Spenlow at the time. I remember the case. Opinion in police circles was that a son of the house was mixed up in it — Jim Abercrombie — awful young waster. Had a pile of debts, and just after the robbery they were all paid off — some rich woman, so they said, but I don't know — Old Abercrombie hedged a bit about the case — tried to call the police off."

"It was just an idea, sir," said Slack.

Miss Marple received Inspector Slack with gratification, especially when she heard that he had been sent by Colonel Melchett.

"Now, really, that is very kind of Colonel Melchett. I didn't know he remembered me."

"He remembers you, all right. Told me that what you didn't know of what goes on in St Mary Mead isn't worth knowing."

"Too kind of him, but really I don't know anything at all. About this murder, I mean."

"You know what the talk about it is."

"Oh, of course — but it wouldn't do, would it, to repeat just idle talk?"

Slack said, with an attempt at geniality, "This isn't an official conversation, you know. It's in confidence, so to speak."

"You mean you really want to know what people are saying? Whether there's any truth in it or not?"

"That's the idea."

"Well, of course, there's been a great deal of talk and speculation. And there are really two distinct camps, if you understand me. To begin with, there are the people who think that the husband did it. A husband or a wife is, in a way, the natural person to suspect, don't you think so?"

"Maybe," said the inspector cautiously.

"Such close quarters, you know. Then, so often, the money angle. I hear that it was Mrs Spenlow who had the money, and therefore Mr Spenlow does benefit by her death. In this wicked world I'm afraid the most uncharitable assumptions are often justified."

"He comes into a tidy sum, all right."

"Just so. It would seem quite plausible, wouldn't it, for him to strangle her, leave the house by the back, come across the fields to my house, ask for me and pretend he'd had a telephone call from me, then go back and find his wife murdered in his absence — hoping, of course, that the crime would be put down to some tramp or burglar."

The inspector nodded. "What with the money angle — and if they'd been on bad terms lately——"

But Miss Marple interrupted him. "Oh, but they hadn't."

"You know that for a fact?"

"Everyone would have known if they'd quarrelled! The maid, Gladys Brent — she'd have soon spread it round the village."

The inspector said feebly. "She mightn't have known——" and received a pitying smile in reply.

Miss Marple went on. "And then there's the other school of thought. Ted Gerard. A good-looking young man. I'm afraid, you know, that good looks are inclined to influence one more than they should. Our last curate but one — quite a magical effect! All the girls came to church — evening service as well as morning. And many older women became unusually active in parish work — and the slippers and scarfs that were made for him! Quite embarrassing for the poor young man.

"But let me see, where was I? Oh, yes, this young man, Ted Gerard. Of course, there has been talk about him. He's come down to see her so often. Though Mrs Spenlow told me herself that he was a member of what I think they call the Oxford Group. A religious movement. They are quite sincere and very earnest, I believe, and Mrs Spenlow was impressed by it all."

Miss Marple took a breath and went on. "And I'm sure there was no reason to believe that there was anything more in it than that, but you know what people are. Quite a lot of people are convinced that Mrs Spenlow was infatuated with the young man, and that she'd lent him quite a lot of money. And it's perfectly true that he was actually seen at the station that day. In the train — the two twenty-seven down train. But of course it would be quite easy, wouldn't it, to slip out of the other side of the train and go through the cutting and over the fence and round by the hedge and never come out of the station entrance at all. So that he need not have been seen going to the cottage. And, of course, people do think that what Mrs Spenlow was wearing was rather peculiar."

"Peculiar?"

"A kimono. Not a dress." Miss Marple blushed. "That sort of thing, you know, is, perhaps, rather suggestive to some people."

"You think it was suggestive?"

"Oh, no, *I* don't think so. I think it was perfectly natural."

"You think it was natural?"

"Under the circumstances, yes." Miss Marple's glance was cool and reflective.

Inspector Slack said, "It might give us another motive for the husband. Jealousy."

"Oh, no. Mr Spenlow would never be jealous. He's not the sort of man who notices things. If his wife had gone away and left a note on the pincushion, it would be the first he'd know of anything of that kind."

Inspector Slack was puzzled by the intent way she was looking at him. He had an idea that all her conversation was intended to hint at something he didn't understand. She said now, with some emphasis, "Didn't *you* find any clues, Inspector — on the spot?"

"People don't leave fingerprints and cigarette ash nowadays Miss Marple."

"But this, I think," she suggested, "was an old-fashioned crime——"

Slack said sharply, "Now what do you mean by that?"

Miss Marple remarked slowly, "I think, you know, that Constable Palk could help you. He was the first person on the — on the 'scene of the crime', as they say."

Mr Spenlow was sitting in a deckchair. He looked bewildered. He said, in his thin, precise voice, "I may, of course, be imagining what occurred. My hearing is not as good as it was. But I distinctly think I heard a small boy call after me, 'Yah, who's a Crippen?' It — it conveyed the impression to me that he was of the opinion that I had — had killed my dear wife."

Miss Marple, gently snipping off a dead rose head, said, "That was the impression he meant to convey, no doubt."

"But what could possibly have put such an idea into a child's head?"

Miss Marple coughed. "Listening, no doubt, to the opinions of his elders."

"You — you really mean that other people think that, also?"

"Quite half the people in St Mary Mead."

"But — my dear lady — what can possibly have given rise to such an idea? I was sincerely attached to my wife. She did not, alas, take to living in the country as much as I had hoped she would do, but perfect agreement on every subject is an impossible idea. I assure you I feel her loss very keenly."

"Probably. But if you will excuse my saying so, you don't sound as though you do."

Mr Spenlow drew his meagre frame up to its full height. "My dear lady, many years ago I read of a certain Chinese philosopher who, when his dearly loved wife was taken from him, continued calmly to beat a gong in the street — a customary Chinese pastime, I presume — exactly as usual. The people of the city were much impressed by his fortitude."

"But," said Miss Marple, "the people of St Mary Mead react rather differently. Chinese philosophy does not appeal to them."

"But you understand?"

Miss Marple nodded. "My Uncle Henry," she explained, "was a man of unusual self-control. His motto was 'Never display emotion'. He, too, was very fond of flowers."

"I was thinking," said Mr Spenlow with something like eagerness, "that I might, perhaps, have a pergola on the west side of the cottage. Pink roses and, perhaps, wisteria. And there is a white starry flower, whose name for the moment escapes me——"

In the tone in which she spoke to her grandnephew, aged three, Miss Marple said, "I have a very nice catalogue here, with pictures. Perhaps you would like to look through it — I have to go up to the village."

Leaving Mr Spenlow sitting happily in the garden with his catalogue, Miss Marple went up to her room, hastily rolled up a dress in a piece of brown paper, and, leaving the house, walked briskly up to the post office. Miss Politt, the dressmaker, lived in rooms over the post office.

But Miss Marple did not at once go through the door and up the stairs. It was just two thirty, and, a minute late, the Much Benham bus drew up outside the post office door. It was one of the events of the day in St Mary Mead. The postmistress hurried out with parcels; parcels connected with the shop side of her business, for the post office also dealt in sweets, cheap books, and children's toys.

For some four minutes, Miss Marple was alone in the post office.

Not till the postmistress returned to her post did Miss Marple go upstairs and explain to Miss Politt that she wanted her old grey crepe altered and made more fashionable if that were possible. Miss Politt promised to see what she could do.

The chief constable was rather astonished when Miss Marple's name was brought to him. She came in with many apologies. "So sorry — so very sorry to disturb you. You are so busy, I know, but then you have always been so very kind, Colonel Melchett, and I felt I would rather come to you instead of to Inspector Slack. For one thing, you know, I should hate Constable Palk to get into any trouble. Strictly speaking, I suppose he shouldn't have touched anything at all."

Colonel Melchett was slightly bewildered. He said, "Palk? That's the St Mary Mead constable, isn't it? What has he been doing?"

"He picked up a pin, you know. It was in his tunic. And it occurred to me at the time that it was quite probable he had actually picked it up in Mrs Spenlow's house."

"Quite, quite. But after all, you know, what's a pin? Matter of fact he did pick the pin up just by Mrs Spenlow's body. Came and told Slack about it yesterday — you put him up to that, I gather? Oughtn't to have touched anything, of course, but as I said, what's a pin? It was only a common pin. Sort of thing any woman might use."

"Oh, no, Colonel Melchett, that's where you're wrong. To a man's eye, perhaps, it looked like an ordinary pin, but it wasn't. It was a special pin, a very thin pin, the kind you buy by the box, the kind used mostly by dressmakers."

Melchett stared at her, a faint light of comprehension breaking in on him. Miss Marple nodded her head several times, eagerly.

"Yes, of course. It seems to me so obvious. She was in her kimono because she was going to try on her new dress, and she went into the front room, and Miss Politt just said something about measurements and put the tape measure round her neck — and then all she'd have to do was to cross it and pull — quite easy, so I've heard. And then, of course, she'd go outside and pull the door to and stand there knocking as though she'd just arrived. But the pin shows she'd *already been in the house*."

"And it was Miss Politt who telephoned to Spenlow?"

"Yes. From the post office at two thirty — just when the bus comes and the post office would be empty."

Colonel Melchett said, "But my dear Miss Marple, why? In heaven's name, why? You can't have a murder without a motive."

"Well, I think, you know, Colonel Melchett, from all I've heard, that the crime dates from a long time back. It reminds me, you know, of my two cousins, Antony and Gordon. Whatever Antony did always went right for him, and with poor Gordon it was just the other way about. Racehorses went lame, and stocks went down, and property depreciated. As I see it, the two women were in it together."

"In what?"

"The robbery. Long ago. Very valuable emeralds, so I've heard. The lady's maid and the tweeny. Because one thing hasn't been explained — how, when the tweeny married the gardener, did they have enough money to set up a flower shop?

"The answer is, it was her share of the — the swag, I think is the right expression. Everything she did turned out well. Money made money. But the other one, the lady's maid, must have been unlucky. She came down to being just a village dressmaker. Then they met again. Quite all right at first, I expect, until Mr Ted Gerard came on the scene.

"Mrs Spenlow, you see, was already suffering from conscience, and was inclined to be emotionally religious. This young man no doubt urged her to 'face up' and to 'come clean' and I daresay she was strung up to do it. But Miss Politt didn't see it that way. All she saw was that she might go to prison for a robbery she had committed years ago. So she made up her mind to put a stop to it all. I'm afraid, you know, that she was always rather a wicked woman. I don't believe she'd have turned a hair if that nice, stupid Mr Spenlow had been hanged."

Colonel Melchett said slowly, "We can — er — verify your theory — up to a point. The identity of the Politt woman with the lady's maid at the Abercrombies', but——"

Miss Marple reassured him. "It will be all quite easy. She's the kind of woman who will break down at once when she's taxed with the truth. And then, you see, I've got her tape measure. I — er — abstracted it yesterday when I was trying on. When she misses it and thinks the police have got it — well, she's quite an ignorant woman and she'll think it will prove the case against her in some way."

She smiled at him encouragingly. "You'll have no trouble, I can assure you." It was the tone in which his favourite aunt had once assured him that he could not fail to pass his entrance examination into Sandhurst.*

And he had passed.

*Sandhurst: a college for army officers

Word List

A

aback (adv) **taken aback** surprised or shocked

abound (v) to be present in large numbers

abruptly (adv) suddenly

abscond (v) to leave suddenly after stealing something

abstract (v) to remove

abstracted (adj) lost in thought

absurd (adj) silly or unreasonable

accomplished (adj) skilful

accord (n) **of your own accord** without being asked or forced to do something

accord (v) to match or agree with something

accordingly (adv) for the reason just given

accustomed (adj) used to

acme (n) **the acme of respectability** the highest level of respectability

acquaint (v) **acquaint someone with** to inform someone about

acquit (v) to give a decision in a court of law that someone is not guilty of a crime

action (n) the process of taking a case to a court of law

acumen (n) the ability to make fast, good judgments

adenoids (n pl) the small pieces of flesh between the back of your nose and throat which, when swollen, cause indistinct speech

administer (v) to give someone a medicine

admonish (v) to tell someone severely that they have done something wrong

adorn (v) to decorate

adroitly (adv) skilfully

affection (n) a feeling of love and caring

affinity (n) close connection

affix (v) to attach

agent (French) a police officer

aghast (adj) shocked

agitation (n) a feeling of being too nervous or upset to think calmly

alas (adv) unfortunately

alert (adj) able to think quickly and notice things

alibi (n) someone or something that proves you were not in the place where a crime was committed

alight (adv) bright

alkaloid (n) an organic chemical compound obtained from plants and often used in drugs

all in (adj) extremely tired

aloud (adv) so that someone can hear

alternate (adj) on one of every two days

ambitious (adj) determined to be rich or successful

amicably (adv) in a friendly way

amongst (prep) among

amply (adv) fully

anew (adv) again

anguish (n) great suffering caused by pain or worry

annual (n) a plant that lives only one year

apologetically (adv) showing that you are sorry for something that you are responsible for

appal (v) to shock

apparel (n) clothes

appraise (v) to judge the value of something

apprehension (n) worry about the future

arouse (v) **arouse jealousy** to make someone feel very jealous; **arouse someone's notice** to make someone become interested

arrogant (adj) so proud of your abilities that you feel more important than others

arsenic (n) a kind of poison, also used for medicinal purposes

artful (adj) clever at deceiving people

ascent (n) climb upwards

ascertain (v) to find out

ashore (adv) on or to the shore

ass (n) a donkey; **make an ass of yourself** to appear foolish

assert (v) to state firmly that something is true

assiduity (n) continued careful attention

astonishment (n) complete surprise

astuteness (n) cleverness

attain (v) to succeed in getting something

attentively (adv) carefully

attribute to (v) to say that someone was responsible for saying or writing something

au fait with (adj) fully informed about

audibly (adv) loud enough to hear

autopsy (n) examination of a dead body to discover the cause of death

avail yourself of (v) to make use of

aversion (n) a strong dislike

avert (v) **avert your eyes** to look away from something that you do not want to see

B

bachelor (n) an unmarried man

badly-off (adj) poor

bagatelle (n) something small and unimportant

baldly (adv) in a way that is true but makes no attempt to be polite

Baron (n) the title of a high-class man

barring (prep) except for

bass (adj) deep and low

battered (adj) covered in marks from long use

bay (n) a tree with sweet-smelling leaves that are used in cooking; **at bay** ready to fight when under attack

bear out (v) to help to prove the truth of something

beaten (adj) **off the beaten track** a place that is not well-known and is far away from the places that people usually visit

bed something out (v) to put plants into the ground

bee (n) a black and yellow flying insect

beehive (n) a structure where **bees** are kept

befall (v) to happen

beforehand (adv) before something else

beneficial (adj) producing desirable results

bequest (n) money or property that you arrange to give to someone after your death

bereavement (n) the fact of losing someone close to you because they have died

between-maid (n) a servant in a large house who helps the cook and other more senior servants

bewildered (adj) confused

bien (French) good

bien sûr (French) of course

blackmail (v) to get money from someone by threatening to tell secrets about them

blessing (n) something that improves your life or makes you happy

bloodstain (n) a mark or spot of blood

blossom (n) a flower or all the flowers on a tree or bush

blotting paper (n) soft thick paper used for drying wet ink on a page

blush (v) to go red in the face, usually with embarrassment

boldness (n) confidence in taking risks and making difficult decisions

bolt (n) a metal bar that you slide across a door to lock it

bolt (v) to run away; to lock with a **bolt**

bon Dieu (French) **le bon Dieu** the good God

bond (n) an official document promising that a government or company will pay back money that it has borrowed

booth (n) **telephone booth** a small structure that contains a public telephone

bound (adj) **bound up in** closely involved; **bound to** very likely to

bow (n/v) the act of bending the top part of your body to greet someone or show respect

brandish (v) to wave threateningly

brass (adj) made from a hard gold-coloured metal

breeze (n) a light wind

bribe (v) to pay money for help, especially with something dishonest

bride (n) a woman at the time she gets married, or just after she is married

bridge (n) a card game

brisk (adj) quick and full of energy

broker (n) a person who buys and sells shares in companies for other people

bronchitis (n) an illness that makes you cough badly

bronze (n) a hard red-brown metal

brooch (n) a piece of jewellery that you fasten to your clothes

brow (n) the part of your face above your eyes and below your hair

brute (n) a rough, cruel man

bulky (adj) big and difficult to carry

bunk (n) a narrow bed on a ship that is fixed to the wall

bureau (n) a large desk

burglar (n) someone who breaks into buildings to steal things

bustle (n) activity with noise and movement

busybody (n) a person who takes too much interest in other people's business

butt in (v) to interrupt

buzz (v) to be noisy with activity and excitement

C

cabin (n) a small room on a ship where you live or sleep

cable (n) a **telegram**

carriage (n) one of the parts of a train where passengers sit; a vehicle with wheels that is pulled by a horse

carry (v) **carry on with** to have a sexual relationship with someone, when you should not

cart (n) a vehicle with two or four wheels that is pulled by a horse

castanets (n pl) a musical instrument made of two pieces of wood that you knock together; **castanets of bronze** an instrument used by Hercules to frighten the birds. As they flew away, he was able to catch them.

casual (adj) happening by chance without being planned

casually (adv) seeming not to care

cause célèbre (French) an event that is discussed with interest by a lot of people

caution (n) **she's a caution** her behaviour is amusing

cautious (adj) careful to avoid danger or risks

certainty (n) the state of being completely sure

certify (v) to state that something is correct, often on an official document

chalk (n) soft white rock often used for writing with

charming (adj) very attractive or pleasing

chasm (n) a deep space between two areas of rock

chime in (v) to add something to a conversation

china (n) a hard white substance produced by baking clay and used to make plates, etc.

chivalry (n) help and protection given to a woman by a man

chlorate (n) a chemical compound

choke someone off (v) to get rid of someone by discouragement

chuckle (v) to laugh quietly

clamour (n) a strong feeling, expressed loudly

claw (n) a sharp nail on the foot of a bird or animal

clean-shaven (adj) without a beard or **moustache**

cliff (n) a high rock with a steep side, near the sea

cloak (n) a loose coat without the pieces which cover your arms

clutch (v) to hold something tightly

coconut (n) the large brown seed of a tropical tree, which has a hard shell containing a white flesh that you can eat and a milky liquid

coincidence (n) a surprising situation in which two things that are connected happen at the same time, in the same place or to the same people

collide (v) to hit something that is moving towards you

Colonel (n) the title of a high-ranking officer in the armed forces

colonial (adj/n) from a country that is under the political control of a more powerful country, but a citizen of the ruling country

comedy (n) a play, etc. that entertains people and makes them laugh

comic (adj) funny

comme ça (French) like that

commence (v) to start

commissaire (French) a senior police officer

commonplace (n) something that is quite usual

compact (n) **powder compact** a small container for face powder

companion (n) someone, especially a woman, who is paid to live or travel with another person; someone you are with on a particular occasion

compelling (adj) making you believe the truth of what is being said

competent (adj) skilful enough to be satisfactory

complacently (adv) in a way that shows you are pleased with yourself

comply (v) to do what you have to do or are asked to do

composed (adj) calm

comprehension (n) understanding

compromising (adj) showing guilt

conceal (v) to hide

conceited (adj) having too high an opinion of your own powers

concierge (French) a receptionist

concrete (adj) definite

condemn (v) to give someone a severe punishment

condescend (v) to do something in a way that shows you think it is below your professional or social position

confederate (n) a person who helps with a crime

confess (v) to admit

confide (v) to tell someone a secret

confidential (adj) trusting someone with information when you do not want other people to know

confoundedly (adv) extremely

conscience (n) your feelings about what is right or wrong; **guilty conscience** feeling very ashamed because you have done something that you know is wrong

conscientiously (adv) with care and attention

constable (n) a low-ranking police officer; **chief constable** an officer in charge of the police in a large area

contemplate (v) to think about something

Continent (n) **the Continent** Western Europe not including Britain

contort (v) to twist violently out of shape

contradictory (adj) completely different from each other

contrary (n) **on the contrary** a phrase used to show that you disagree with a previous statement, showing that the opposite is true

contrive (v) to arrange something in a clever way, especially secretly or by deceiving people

convalescent (adj) getting well after an illness

conversant (adj) **conversant with** familiar with

convey (v) to communicate information or a message

convulse (v) to shake violently

cook (v) **cook the books** to dishonestly change official records

copingstone (n) the final item that completes something

copper-coloured (adj) reddish-brown

cord (v) to tie up with thin rope

cork (n) a light material from the outside of some trees that floats in water

correspondence (n) letters received and sent

corrupt (adj) dishonest

Countess (n) the title of a high-class woman

coup (n) an achievement that is extremely impressive because it was very difficult

coward (n) someone who is not at all brave

credentials (n pl) proof of your identity or your achievements

credulous (adj) easily deceived because you trust people

crepe (n) soft, thin cloth

crestfallen (adj) very disappointed

crisply (adv) quickly and confidently

crop off (v) to cut off part of something

cross-examination (n) a serious and detailed questioning

croyez-moi (French) believe me

crumb (n) a very small piece of food

crystal gazer (n) someone who looks into a glass ball to see the future

curate (n) an assistant priest

curiosity (n) a desire to know something

curious (adj) strange or unusual; wanting to know about something

curse (v) to ask God to harm someone

cutting (n) a passage cut through rising ground for a railway line

D

d'abord (French) first

damn (v) to state that something is very bad; to show that you are extremely angry with someone or something

damnably (adv) terribly

damned (adv) annoying

damning (adj) something that shows someone or something is very bad

dangle (v) to hang loosely

daresay (v) I daresay used when saying that something may perhaps be true

darn (adj) terrible or stupid

dart (v) to move suddenly and quickly

dash (v) to run quickly

deceased (n) a dead person

decisively (adv) with confidence

deckchair (n) a folding chair with a long seat made of cloth

decompose (v) to make something divide into smaller parts

decoy away (v) to trick someone into leaving

deduce (v) to make a judgment based on information or experience

defaulting (adj) a person who does not do what he is legally supposed to do

defiant (adj) showing no fear

deft (adj) quick and skilful

defy (v) to refuse to obey

delight (v) to be very pleased to

delirious (adj) extremely excited or happy

depart (v) to leave

depreciate (v) to decrease in value

descend (v) to go down

despair (n) a feeling of great unhappiness without hope that a situation will improve

despatch (v) to send

despise (v) to dislike very much

detachment (n) a lack of personal feeling

detain (v) to keep back

detest (v) to hate

devoid (adj) **devoid of** without

devoted (adj) showing great love and loyalty

devour (v) to eat something quickly

dew (n) small wet drops

dexterity (n) the ability to be quick and skilful, usually with your hands

diffidently (adv) **hesitatingly**, without self-confidence

dignity (n) calm behaviour that shows self-respect, even in difficult situations

dim (adj) fairly dark

dim (v) to become less bright

diminish (v) to become smaller or less important

dine (v) to eat dinner

dip (v) to put something into a liquid or powder and take it out again quickly; **penny dip (**n) a game costing a penny. You put your hand in a container of small objects and choose one without looking.

discharge (v) to fire (a gun)

discreet (adj) careful not to say too much; polite

discretion (n) the ability not to offend or embarrass people

disdain to (v) to be too proud to do something

disfavour (n) a feeling of dislike and disapproval

disguise (n) something that you wear to hide your appearance or identity

dishevelled (adj) very untidy

dispensary (n) a place where medicine is prepared

dispenser (n) someone who mixes and prepares medicines

disposal (n) the act of getting rid of something

dissect (v) to examine something in great detail

dissolve (v) to make something solid become part of a liquid by putting it in a liquid and mixing it

distract (v) to prevent someone from continuing with what they are doing by making them look at or listen to something else

distracted (adj) unable to think clearly

distraction (n) **drive someone to distraction** to make someone extremely angry or upset

distraught (adj) extremely upset

distress (n/v) great unhappiness

disturb (v) to interrupt

disturbed (adj) shocked and worried

dive (v) to move quickly and suddenly

divorce (n) the legal ending of a marriage

do (v) **do in, do away with** to murder

docteur (French) doctor

dodge (v) to avoid something by quick movement

dole (n) money given by the government to unemployed people

doll (n) a child's toy that looks like a person

dovetail (v) to fit together

down (adv) **go down with** to have a particular illness

drain from (v) to leave

drastic (adj) strong, sudden and often severe

drawing room (n) a room where you can entertain guests or relax, especially in a large house

drawn (adj) thin and pale as a result of illness or worry

dreadful (adj) very unpleasant

dressing gown (n) a long, loose coat that you wear in your house, often over **pyjamas**

droning (adj) low and dull

droop (n) hanging down

duly (adv) as expected

dumbfounded (adj) very surprised

dummy (n) an object made to look like a real thing

dunno don't know

duplicate (n/adj) an exact copy

dusk (n) the time before it gets dark

dwell (v) to live; **dwell on** to continue to think about

dye (v) to change the colour of something using a substance called **dye**

E

eagle (n) a very large bird that eats small animals and birds; **with an eagle glance** very good at seeing and noticing things

earnest (adj) serious

ease (n) an easy way; **life of ease** a comfortable life

eccentric (adj) unusual

eh bien (French) well

ejaculate (v) to say something suddenly

elated (adj) extremely happy

elder (adj) older

elicit (v) to succeed in getting information from someone

elite (n) the most important people in a social group

elusive (adj) difficult to find

embark upon (v) to start

embezzlement (n) dishonest use of money that you are responsible for

emerald (n) a valuable bright green stone

eminently (adv) extremely

en avant (French) forward

en route to (prep) on the way to

enamel (n) a shiny substance that is put onto metal for decoration or protection

encounter (v) to meet

endeavour (n/v) attempt

enfin (French) at last; in fact

engaging (adj) attracting attention and interest

engineer (v) to bring about

enigmatically (adv) mysteriously

enlarge (adv) to make something bigger

enlighten (v) to explain something to someone

enrage (v) to make someone angry

entail (v) to make it necessary to do something

entrench (v) to establish firmly

entrust (v) to make someone responsible for something important

enumerate (v) to list things

even (adj) not changing

evolution (n) a gradual change and development

exacting (adj) demanding a lot of effort

exaggerate (v) to make something seem more important than it is

excessively (adv) more than is reasonable or necessary

exclaim (v) to speak suddenly and loudly

exclamation (n) a sudden, loud word or phrase

execute (v) to perform

exert (v) to use your influence

exhaustion (n) extreme tiredness

exhume (v) to take a dead body out of a grave

exile (n) **go into exile** to go and live in another country because you are forced to leave your own

exotic (adj) unusual and exciting because of its foreign connection

exterminate (v) to kill large numbers of animals or people so that there are no more of that type

extract (v) to remove

extradition (n) the legal process of returning someone to another country where they are thought to be a criminal

extravagant (adj) extreme

eye (n) **my eye** nonsense

eyebrow (n) the line of hair above your eye

F

facetious (adj) saying things that are intended to be clever and funny but are really silly and annoying

falter (v) to become weaker and less certain; to move unsteadily

fancywork (n) decorative sewing

fantastic (adj) very strange

farewell (n) goodbye; **bid farewell** to say goodbye

fascinate (v) to interest someone greatly

fatal (adj) resulting in death

fate (n) a power that is believed to control what happens in people's lives

fatigued (adj) tired

fed up (adj) annoyed or bored, and wanting something to change

feebly (adv) weakly

fence (n) a structure made of wood or metal, etc.; someone who buys and sells stolen goods

fend someone off (v) to defend yourself against someone

fender (n) a low metal wall around a fireplace

fern (n) a kind of green plant

fete (n) an outdoor event where there are competitions, etc., organised to get money

fiancée (n) a woman who is engaged to be married

fibre (n) **of loose moral fibre** not completely honest

fiddle (v) **fiddle round with** to keep moving or making changes to things

fishmonger (n) a shopkeeper who sells fish

flag (n) a smooth, flat piece of stone used for paths, floors, etc.

flap (v) to move up and down

flattered (adj) pleased

flicker (v) to shine or burn with a light that goes on and off quickly; to make a sudden series of movements

fling (v) to throw

flirtatious (adj) with a suggestion of sexual interest

florist (n) someone who sells flowers

flourish (n) with a large, confident movement

flourish (v) to develop well and be successful

flush (v) to go red in the face

fluster (v) to make someone nervous and confused

fly (n) a carriage pulled by one horse

forbidding (adj) unfriendly and dangerous-looking

foreboding (n) a feeling of something bad to come

forfeit (v) to lose as a result of breaking an agreement

forsake (v) to give up

forth (adv) **pull forth** to pull out

forthwith (adv) immediately

fortitude (n) courage

foul (adj) horrible

frankness (n) honesty and openness

fretful (adj) anxious and complaining

fright (n) a feeling of fear

frightful (adj) unpleasant

frightfully (adv) extremely

fro (adv) **to and fro** in one direction and then back again

frown (v) to move your eyebrows together in an angry or unhappy expression

fry (v) to cook in hot oil

funk (v) to avoid doing something that is difficult or that frightens you

furtive (adj) secretive

fuss (v) to worry too much about things that are not very important

G

gaiety (n) **gaieties** enjoyable activities

gaily (adv) in a happy, cheerful way

gallant (adj) brave

galling (adj) unfair, making you feel upset and angry

gamble (v) **gamble on** to take a risk that a course of action will succeed

gamut (n) the complete range of possibilities

garish (adj) too brightly coloured

gasp (n/v) a sudden, noisy taking-in of breath

gastric (adj) of the stomach; **gastric ulcer** a sore area in your stomach that may bleed or produce poisonous juices

gauge (v) to calculate

gaunt (adj) thin and unattractive

gay (adj) cheerful and excited

gaze (v) to look at something for a long time

geniality (n) cheerful friendliness

genius (n) someone with a very high level of ability

genteel (adj) trying to appear of a high social class

gesticulate (v) to make movements with your arms or hands

gifted (adj) with a natural ability for something

gingerly (adv) very carefully

gleam (n) a small, pale light

glibly (adv) easily, without thinking

glimmering (n) a small sign of thought or feeling

gloomily (adv) sadly, without hope that a situation will improve

glory (n) honour and praise

gong (n) a round metal object which makes a loud noise when struck

goods (n pl) **he's the goods** he has real quality

gossip (n/v) talk about the details of other people's private lives

governess (n) a female teacher who lives with a rich family and teaches their children at home

graduated (adj) of different levels

grandnephew (n) a son of a child of your brother or sister

gratification (n) satisfaction

gravity (n) seriousness

grease (n) animal fat or any thick oily substance

greedy (adj) wanting more money, power, food, etc.

grim (adj) serious and worried; unpleasant and unattractive

grimace (n) an expression of dislike or pain

grin (v) to smile widely

grip (n/v) a tight hold

grippe (French) **la grippe** an infectious disease like a bad cold, **influenza**

groan (v) to make a long, deep sound of pain or disappointment

grounds (n pl) a reason

grudge (v) to be unwilling for someone to have something

gruesome (adj) horrible

guileless (adj) honest, without trying to hide anything

guinea (n) the sum of one pound one **shilling**

H

haggard (adj) having lines on your face and dark marks around your eyes especially from tiredness, worry or illness

hail (v) to greet

half a crown (n) the sum of two **shillings** and sixpence (thirty pence)

halting (adj) slow, with pauses

handkerchief (n) a cloth for drying your nose or eyes

handsome (adj) good-looking; **a handsome price** a large amount of money

hard up (adj) poor

harmoniously (adv) without disagreeing or fighting

harpy (n) a creature in old stories, half woman, half bird, very greedy and cruel

harrowing (adj) very frightening or shocking

haughty (adj) proud and unfriendly

haute noblesse (French) people of a high social class

headline (n) the title of a newspaper report

hearthrug (n) a small carpet that lies in front of a fire in a house

hearty (adj) large

hedge (n) a row of small bushes dividing one field or garden from another

hedge (v) to refuse to answer directly

heed (n) attention

heels (n pl) **take to your heels** to start running as fast as possible

henna (n) a natural substance used to change your hair colour to a reddish-brown

heroine (n) the woman who is the main character in a story, play, etc.

hesitant (adj) uncertain how to act

hesitate (v) to pause before speaking or acting

hiker (n) someone on a walking holiday

hinge (v) **hinge on** to depend on

hint (n/v) an indirect message

hoarse (adj) a **hoarse** voice sounds rough, as if the speaker has a sore throat

horrified (adj) shocked

hors de combat (French) unable to fight

housekeeper (n) someone who is employed to manage the housework in a home or hotel

hum (v) to be very busy and full of activity

humdrum (adj) very ordinary

hush up (v) to keep something secret

hydra (n) a snake in ancient Greek stories which has many heads that grow again when they are cut off

I

identical (adj) exactly the same

idle (adj) **idle talk** casual conversation without purpose

ignorant (adj) not knowing facts or information that you ought to know

illuminating (adj) **illuminating answer** an answer that makes things clear

immobile (adj) not moving at all

impatience (n) annoyance at delays or weakness

imperative (adj) extremely important and urgent

impersonator (n) someone who pretends to be another person

imperturbable (adj) calm and unworried

implicitly (adv) completely

impulse (n) a sudden strong desire to act

inadvertently (adv) by accident

incisively (adv) clearly and directly

inclined (adj) ready

incognito (adj) without telling people who you really are

incoherence (n) expressing thoughts, ideas, etc. badly so that they are difficult to understand

inconspicuous (adj) not noticeable

incredible (adj) unbelievable

incredulity (n) a feeling that you cannot believe something

incredulous (adj) unable to believe something

indifference (n) a lack of interest or caring

indignation (n) a feeling of surprise and anger

indulge (v) to enjoy; **indulge someone** let someone have or do whatever they want

infatuated (adj) with unreasonable feelings of love

inflammation (n) a swelling or soreness in or on part of your body

influenza (n) an infectious disease like a bad cold

ingenuity (n) cleverness in thinking of new ideas

inherit (v) to receive money or property from someone after their death

inkling (n) a slight idea

inmate (n) a person living in a building

inn (n) a small hotel with a bar

innocent (adj) not guilty of a crime

inquisitive (adj) anxious to find out about the details of something

insanely (adv) madly

inscription (n) a piece of writing

insistently (adv) firmly and repeatedly

instantly (adv) immediately

instinct (n) a natural tendency to behave or react in a certain way

intelligible (adj) understandable

intent (adj) paying careful attention

interfere (v) to deliberately get involved in a situation that does not concern you

interior (n) the inside of a house, etc.

interrogate (v) to ask a lot of questions to get information from someone

intimacy (n) the state of having a close personal relationship

intonation (n) the way you change the levels of your voice to add meaning to your speech

invade (v) to interrupt in an annoying way

invalid (n) a person who cannot look after themselves because of illness, old age or injury

inveterate (adj) **inveterate talker** someone who talks a lot and cannot stop

irritably (adv) showing annoyance

irritated (adj) annoyed

J

jam down (v) to push something down hard

jamais de la vie! (French) absolutely not!

jest (n) a joke

jolly (adj) cheerful

jubilant (adj) joyful and **triumphant**

jumper (n) a piece of clothing made of wool without buttons that you wear over a shirt

junction (n) a place where one railway line joins another

K

keep (v) **keep your head** to stay calm in a difficult situation

kidney (n) one or more of the two organs from the lower back of an animal that separates waste liquid from your blood, used as food

kimono (n) a long, loose, typically Japanese piece of clothing like a thin coat

knit (v) to make clothes out of wool

L

labyrinth (n) a complicated network

lace (n) fine cloth made with patterns of small holes

lachrymose (adj) often crying

lame (adj) unable to walk properly because your leg is injured

landlady (n) a woman that you rent a room or building from

lantern-jawed (adj) with a long, narrow jaw and cheeks that sink inwards

leak out (v) if secret information **leaks out** a lot of people find out about it

leap (v) to jump

legacy (n) money or property that you receive from someone after they die

legend (n) an old, well-known story

level-headed (adj) calm and sensible in making decisions

lid (n) **put the lid on** to do something that finally ruins or ends someone's plans or hopes

light upon (v) to find something by accident

light-headed (adj) unable to think clearly or move steadily

limb (n) an arm or leg

liner (n) a large passenger ship

linguist (n) someone who is good at foreign languages or knows about language

liqueur (n) a sweet, strong alcoholic drink

loch (n) a Scottish lake

lodge (n) a small house on the land of a large country house

lodge (v) to pay someone rent so you can live in a room in their house

lodger (n) someone who pays rent to live in a house with its owner

logical (adj) reasonable and sensible

loop (v) to move something in a circular direction and fasten it

lounge (n) a sitting room

lurk (v) to wait somewhere quietly and secretly

luxuriantly (adv) strongly and thickly

M

ma'am (n) a short form of *madam*

madonna (n) a picture or figure of Mary, the mother of Jesus

maid (n) a female servant, usually in a large house

maiden (n) **maiden name** the family name that a woman had before she got married

mais non (French) but no

mais oui (French) but yes

make-up (n) substances such as powder, creams, etc. that some people put on their faces to improve or change their appearance; the qualities, attitudes, etc. in someone's character

mal de mer (French) seasickness

malicious (adj) showing a desire to hurt someone

manslaughter (n) the crime of killing someone without intending to

mantelpiece (n) a shelf above a fireplace

marble (n) a hard, usually white rock that becomes smooth when it is polished and that is used in buildings

mare (n) **mare's nest** a discovery which turns out to be imaginary

margarine (n) a yellow substance like butter but not made from milk

maternal (adj) **maternal grandmother** your mother's mother

matrimony (n) the state of marriage

meagre (adj) thin, small

medium (adj) middle-sized

medium (n) someone who claims to have the power to receive messages from the dead

meekly (adv) gently

melancholy (adj) sad

melodramatic (adj) with dramatic emphasis

mercilessly (adv) without kindness or forgiveness

Messrs (n pl) the plural of Mr, used especially in the names of companies

midst (n) **in their midst** among them

mildly (adv) slightly

minute (adj) paying careful attention to the smallest details

Missus (n) a way of addressing a woman without using her name

mistress (n) the female employer of servants

mocking (adj) showing unkind amusement

moderately (adv) quite

modestly (adv) without pride

mon ami (French) my friend

mon cher (French) my dear

monied (adj) rich

monopolise (v) to demand a lot of someone's time and attention

monster (n) a cruel and evil creature

moor (n) an open area of high land covered in rough grass or low bushes

morrow (n) **on the morrow** the next day

motive (n) a reason for doing something

motto (n) a short statement of aims or beliefs

mount (v) to hang; to go up; to increase gradually

moustache (n) hair that grows on a man's upper lip

muddle (n) confusion

muffle (v) to wrap tightly

murmur (v) to speak in a soft, low voice

mutter (v) to speak in a low, unclear voice

mystified (adj) unable to understand or explain

N

namesake (n) another person with the same name

narrate (v) to tell a story

narrative (n) a story

native (adj) **native language** a person's first language

neglect (v) to not look after someone or something properly

negotiable (adj) that can be exchanged for money

nemesis (n) a fair punishment brought to you by **fate**

nephew (n) a son of your brother or sister

nibble (v) to eat by taking very small bites

nick (n) **in the nick of time** just in time

nightmare (n) a terrible dream or experience

nitrate (n) a chemical compound

noncommittal (adj) not expressing a definite opinion

notify (v) to inform someone about something

notorious (adj) famous for something bad

novelty (n) the quality of being new or unusual

noxious (adj) unpleasant

O

oak (n) a kind of tree or wood from this tree

oblige (v) to force someone; **be obliged** to be pleased; **obliging** willing and eager to help

obscure (adj) not very well-known or important

obstinately (adv) refusing to change your mind or behaviour

occasional (adj) happening sometimes but not often

odd (adj) **forty-odd** a little more than forty

omen (n) a sign that something is going to happen; **of ill omen** which is a sign of future trouble

omit (v) to not include something either deliberately or because you forget to do it

opera (n) a musical play in which all the words are sung

optimism (n) a tendency to believe that good things will happen

orthodox (adj) normal and correct

outing (n) a short trip, usually by a group of people and for pleasure

overboard (adv) over the side of a boat and into the water

overdose (n) too much of a drug taken at one time

overhear (v) to hear other people's conversation by accident

overlook (n) to not notice something

overreach yourself (v) to try to do more than you are capable of doing

overstrain (n) too much worry

overtake (v) to happen to you, suddenly preventing you from following your own plans; to go past a person because you are going faster than them

overwhelming (adj) too strong to resist

P

pageboy (n) a boy servant in a hotel

painstaking (adj) very careful and thorough

palatable (adj) agreeable

palm (n) a tropical tree with a long straight trunk and large pointed leaves at the top

palpable (adj) clearly noticeable

pang (n) a sudden feeling of fear, pain, etc.

pant (v) to breathe quickly after taking exercise

parlance (n) a particular way of speaking

parlourmaid (n) a female servant who is employed to clean rooms, etc. in a large house

parry (v) to defend yourself against attack, or to avoid answering difficult questions

pasteboard (n) flat, stiff card made by sticking sheets of paper together

pastime (n) an activity that you enjoy doing in your free time

pathetically (adv) in a way that makes you feel pity

patronise (v) to use a shop, etc.

peach (n) a round, sweet, juicy fruit with a soft yellow or red skin

pearl (n) a small, shiny, white jewel

peculiar (adj) strange

pedigree (n) an origin which is known

peer (v) to look very carefully, usually because something is difficult to see

penetrate (v) to enter or pass through something

perennial (n) a plant that lives for many years

perfunctory (adj) quick and without much care

pergola (n) a high frame over which plants can grow

perplexedly (adv) showing worry or confusion

persecutor (n) someone who continues to harm a person

persevere (v) to continue trying to do something that is difficult

personage (n) an important person

personified (adj) in person

perspiration (n) liquid that appears on your skin when it is hot

persuasively (adv) in a way that hopes to persuade someone

perusal (n) reading

petrified (adj) in a state of shock or fear which prevents movement

petulant (adj) childishly impatient and angry for no reason

pillar (n) a tall, round post often used to support a roof

pillow (n) a bag of soft material that you rest your head on when you sleep

pinch (v) to steal

pincushion (n) a soft, filled bag used for sticking pins in when you do not need them

pine (n) a tree with long sharp leaves that do not fall off in winter

piqued (adj) annoyed and offended

placid (adj) calm

plausible (adj) reasonable and likely to be true

plucky (adj) brave

plunge (v) **make a plunge** to begin to do something suddenly, without thinking about the possible results

poise (n) self-confidence and self-control

poke (v) **poke round** to look for something by moving a lot of things around

pommade (French) an oil that men rub into their hair to make it smooth

porch (n) an entrance to a building, outside the front door, covered by a roof

porter (n) someone in charge of the entrance to a hotel

portmanteau (n) a travelling case, trunk

postmistress (n) a woman who runs a post office

post-mortem (n) an examination of a dead body to find out the cause of death

postpone (v) to change an event to a later time

potassium cyanide (n) a poison which kills immediately

pottery (n) objects made out of baked clay

practicable (adj) useful in a particular situation

precious (adj) valuable or very important

precipitate (v) to separate a solid substance from a liquid by chemical action

précisément (French) exactly

predecessor (n) someone who had your job before you

prejudice (n) an unreasonable distrust of people

pretext (n) an excuse

prey (n) **bird of prey** a bird that kills other birds and animals for food

prim (adj) small and neat

prise (v) to force

privacy (n) the state of being alone, without the attention of others

prodigal (adj) **prodigal son** a son who behaves badly, but is then sorry about his behaviour

profess (v) to claim feelings or beliefs that you do not have

professor (n) a university teacher of the highest rank

prognostication (n) a statement about what will happen

prompt (adj) done quickly, immediately

prop up (v) to support

prophesy (v) to say what will happen in the future

prosper (v) to be successful and become rich

proverbial (adj) well-known by a lot of people

prowl (v) to move quietly around an area while hunting

puff (n) praise intended to increase sales

puff out (v) to fill with air and become bigger

pull (v) **pull someone's leg** to make a joke by telling someone something that is not actually true

punctilious (adj) very careful

pursed (adj) drawn together

pursuant (adj) **pursuant to** according to

puzzle (n) something that is difficult to explain or understand

puzzled (adj) confused and unable to understand

pyjamas (n pl) a soft pair of trousers and a top that you wear in bed

Q

quarry (n) a person or animal which is being hunted

quarter (n) **close quarters** very near

quavering (adj) with a shaking, unsteady sound

quay (n) a place where boats stop to load and unload

queer (adj) strange

quick-witted (adj) able to understand things quickly

quiver (v) to shake, tremble

R

rake (v) **rake something up** to talk about something from the past that people would prefer you not to mention

rage (n) a strong feeling of uncontrollable anger

railing (n) one of the upright bars in a metal fence

rampart (n) a wide wall of stone or earth built to protect a castle or city

rap (v) to knock quickly and lightly

rash (adj) doing something too quickly, without careful thought about whether it is sensible

readjust (v) to put back into position

reasonable (adj) fair and sensible

reassure (v) to make someone feel less worried about a situation

recall (v) to remember

recompense (v) to give someone a reward for their help or trouble

recount (v) to tell

rectory (n) the house where the priest in charge of a parish lives

recur (v) to be repeated again and again

red-handed (adj) in the act of committing a crime

references (n pl) letter(s) of recommendation

refute (v) to say or prove that a statement is wrong

regret (n/v) sadness about something because you are sorry that it happened

reiterate (v) to repeat

relapse (v) to return to previous bad habits

reluctance (n) unwillingness

remarkable (adj) unusual or surprising

render (v) **render someone incapable** to make someone unable to do something

repentance (n) the state of being sorry for something you have done

repetition (n) saying the same thing many times

repose (n) rest

reprove (v) to criticise

requisition (v) to hire, rent

resemblance (n) a similarity in the appearance of two people or things

resent (v) to feel angry about

reside (v) to live in a particular place

residue (n) the remaining part of something

resolute (adj) determined, because you have strong beliefs, aims, etc.

resort (n) **as a last resort** when everything else fails

resourceful (adj) able to find a way around difficulties

respectable (adj) with accepted standards of behaviour

resume (v) **resume your seat** to go back to the seat where you were before

retrieve (v) to find something and bring it back

revolve (v) to spin around

revolver (n) a small gun

rigorous (adj) careful and exact

ripe (adj) ready to eat; **the moment/time is ripe for** it is a suitable time to do something

robustly (adv) in a strong and determined way

romance (n) love, or a feeling of being in love

rouge (n) red powder or cream that women put on their cheeks

roundabout (adj) not done in the shortest, most direct way possible

ruefully (adv) regretfully

rugged (adj) rough and uneven

rumour (n) information that is passed from one person to another and which may or may not be true

S

sachet (n) a small bag

sanity (n) the condition of being mentally healthy

sapristi! (French) a word used to express great surprise

saucer (n) a small round plate that curves up at the edges that you put a cup on

saunter (v) to walk in a slow, unhurried way

scan (v) to read something quickly

scandal (n) behaviour or events that you consider to be shocking

scarf (n) a long, narrow piece of material that you wear around your neck

scent (n) a pleasant-smelling liquid that you put on your skin

sceptical (adj) doubtful about the truth of what you are told

scone (n) a small, round cake

scornful (adj) showing that you think an idea is stupid

scotch (v) **scotch a rumour** to stop people saying something untrue

scrap (n) a small piece

scratch (v) to make a mark or cut on a hard surface

scream (n/v) a loud, high sound that you make with your voice when you are frightened

scribble (v) to write quickly

scrutinise (v) to examine something carefully

seal (v) to close a package, envelope, etc. by using something sticky to hold its edges in place

securities (n pl) financial documents such as **bonds**

seldom (adv) very rarely

sensation (n) a feeling

sensational (adj) exciting

sensationalism (n) a way of reporting events that make them seem as shocking or exciting as possible

serene (adj) calm and relaxed

set up (adj) healthy

setback (n) something that delays progress

shady (adj) of doubtful honesty

shampoo (v) to wash with liquid soap

shawl (n) a piece of soft cloth that people, especially women, wear around their shoulders or head

shed (v) **shed light on** to make something easier to understand

sheer (adj) pure

sheer (v) **sheer off** to change direction suddenly, especially in order to avoid something

shilling (n) a coin which was formerly a unit of British money (twelve pence)

shiver (n/v) a slight shaking movement caused by cold or fear

shooting box (n) a small house in the country, used by hunters

shrink from (v) to avoid doing something difficult or unpleasant

shrug (v) to raise your shoulders, expressing doubt or lack of interest

shudder (n) shaking with fear or horror

shy (v) to throw a ball at something; **coconut shy** a game in which you try to knock **coconuts** off posts by throwing balls at them

sigh (v) to breathe making a long sound that shows you are sad, disappointed, tired or relieved

sip (v) to drink something slowly, taking small mouthfuls

situated (adj) **be situated** to be in a particular position or place

skirt (v) to go round

slander (n) a false statement about someone with the intention of making others think badly of them

sleek (adj) smooth and shining

slender (adj) thin and graceful

slip (n) a mistake

slippers (n pl) soft shoes that you wear at home

sly (adj) clever in the use of tricks and dishonesty

smuggle (v) to take into a country secretly and unlawfully

snatch (v) to take something with a quick, violent movement

sneak (v) to take secretly

sniff (v) to breathe air into your nose noisily, especially in short breaths

snip (v) to cut something quickly with scissors

snort (v) to express anger, impatience or amusement by breathing air noisily through your nose

sob (v) to cry noisily

soberly (adv) seriously

solemnly (adv) with great seriousness

solicitude (n) anxious care

soothe (v) to make someone less anxious

spanner (n) **car spanner** a metal tool used for taking a wheel off a car

spare (adj) thin

spate (n) a large amount

spectacles (n pl) glasses

speculation (n) the act of guessing without having much information

spill (v) to make a liquid flow over the edge of a container by accident

spine (n) the row of bones down the centre of your back

spinster (n) an unmarried woman

spiritualism (n) the belief that dead people may send messages to living people

splendid (adj) very fine

sprawl (v) to lie or sit with your arms or legs stretched out in a careless way

sprint (v) to run fast

spruce (adj) neat and clean

squire (n) the main landowner in a village

squirrel (n) a small animal with a thick tail

stagger (v) to walk unsteadily, almost falling over

stammer (v) to speak with pauses and repeated sounds because you are nervous

standoffish (adj) rather unfriendly and formal

startled (adj) suddenly surprised or slightly shocked

steak (n) good quality beef

steam (n) **blow off steam** to release feelings you have stopped yourself from showing

stentorian (adj) loud and strong

stepfather (n) a man who is married to your mother but is not your father

stewed (adj) cooked slowly in water

stingy (adj) not at all generous, especially with money

stint (v) to give or use too little of something

stipulate (v) to demand as a condition

stir (v) to move slightly

stock (n) a share in a company, or the value of that share

stodgy (adj) dull

stolid (adj) not showing any emotion or feeling

stoop (v) to bend your body forwards and down

stout (adj) quite fat and heavy

strangle (v) to kill by pressing on the throat

straw (n) **catch at a straw** to attempt to solve a difficulty by means that are unlikely to succeed

stray (adj) accidently separated from others

strive (v) to try hard

stroll (n/v) a slow, relaxed walk

strung up (adj) **strung up to do something** feeling so guilty that you are ready to do something

subdued (adj) quiet

substitute (v) to replace one person or thing with another

successive (adj) following one after the other

suicide (n) the act of killing yourself

sullen (adj) silently showing anger or bad temper

sum up (v) to end with a statement of the main information

summon (v) to order someone to attend

sundry (n) **all and sundry** everyone, not just particular people

superior (adj) feeling that you are better than others

superstitious (adj) influenced by beliefs about luck and magic

suppress (v) to hide

surmise (n) a guess based on what you know already

suspicion (n) a feeling that someone is probably guilty of something wrong or dishonest

swag (n) goods obtained in a robbery

sway (v) to move unsteadily from side to side

swerve (v) to turn to one side

swiftly (adv) quickly

T

tabby (n) a type of cat

tack (n) a line of action

tact (n) careful politeness so that you do not upset someone

tally (v) to agree or equal exactly

talon (n) a sharp curved nail on the feet of some birds that catch animals

tangible (adj) clear

tariff (n) a list of prices

tax someone with (v) to blame someone for something

telegram (n) a message sent by using radio or electrical signals

telegraph (v) to send a message using radio or electrical signals

temple (n) the side of the head

tempt (v) to make someone want to do something

tentatively (adv) uncertainly, without much confidence

term (n) **be on good/bad terms** to have a friendly/bad relationship with someone

terrace (n) an area outside a building where you can sit, often to eat or drink

terrified (adj) extremely afraid

theft (n) the crime of stealing

thereupon (adv) immediately after something else

thrilled (adj) pleased and excited

thrust (n) a sudden strong movement forward; the main meaning of what someone says

thrust (v) to push with a sudden or violent movement

thump (n/v) a heavy sound of something hitting a surface

tiara (n) a piece of jewellery like a small crown

tidy (adj) **a tidy sum** a large amount of money

tiresome (adj) annoying

tisane (French) a kind of tea made from dried plants

to-do (n) unnecessary excitement about something

toothcomb (n) **go over with a toothcomb** to search very thoroughly

toss up (n) an equal chance

trace (n) a small sign that something existed

trace (v) to find someone or something after a careful search

tragedy (n) a very sad event

trait (n) a particular quality in someone's character

tramp (n) a person without a home or job, who lives outside and often asks for food or money

trample (v) to step heavily on something

transatlantic (adj) crossing the Atlantic Ocean

transpire (v) to become known

très bien (French) very good

trickle (v) to move slowly in a thin stream

trifling (adj) of small importance; **a trifle** slightly

trim (v) to cut something to make it neater

trite (adj) unoriginal, so it sounds insincere

triumphantly (adv) expressing pleasure at your success

trivial (adj) unimportant

try (v) to examine and judge someone in a court who is thought to be guilty of a crime

trying (adj) annoying or difficult

tug (n) a small, strong boat used for pulling or guiding ships into a port

tunic (n) a short coat worn by policeman

turn (v) **not turn a hair** to remain completely calm when something bad or surprising suddenly happens

tweeny (n) a low-level servant, assistant to the cook and the **parlourmaid**

twin (n) one of two children born at the same time to the same mother

twinkle (n/v) an expression in your eyes that shows you are amused or happy

twitch (v) to make a sudden, uncontrolled movement

twopenny-halfpenny/tuppenny-ha'penny (adj) of very little value

type (n) printed letters

U

umbrella (n) a frame covered in cloth that you hold above your head to protect you from the rain

'un (n) **wrong 'un** a bad person

unaccountable (adj) difficult to explain

unassuming (adj) showing no desire for attention or special treatment

uncongenial (adj) unpleasant

underexposed (adj) without enough light to allow a clear photograph

under-secretaryship (n) an important political position in charge of a government department

undignified (adj) embarrassing because you look silly

undoubtedly (adv) without doubt

unencumbered with (adj) free from

unexacting (adj) demanding little effort or skill

unfathomable (adj) too strange or mysterious to understand

unforeseen (adj) unexpected

unlatch (v) to unlock by lifting a small metal bar

unobtrusive (adj) not attracting attention

unreliable (adj) unable to be trusted or depended upon

usher in (v) to show someone the way into a place

utmost (n) **do your utmost** to try as hard as you can to achieve something

utter (v) to say something

utterly (adv) completely

V

vague (adj) unclear

vaguely (adv) in a way that shows you are not thinking about what you are doing

valet (n) a personal manservant

vanish (v) to disappear

vehement (adj) showing very strong feelings

veil (v) to cover something with a thin piece of material

venomous (adj) full of hatred

verdict (n) an official decision about whether a person is guilty or not of a crime

verify (v) to find out if something is true

veritable (adj) true (a word used to emphasise the correctness of a comparison)

verity (n) truth

vicarage (n) a house where a priest in charge of a parish lives

vicinity (n) the area around a particular place

vigorously (adv) with a lot of energy or determination

vile (adj) very unpleasant

vindicate (v) to prove that someone is not guilty

vinegar-tongued (adj) unkind in speech

vista (n) the possibility of new ideas, events, etc.

visualise (v) to form a picture of something in your mind

vitality (n) great energy

vociferous (adj) noisy in expressing your feelings

volition (n) **without volition** without wanting to

voyage (v) a journey by ship

voyons (French) let's see; look!

vulture (n) a large bird which feeds on dead animals; a person who pitilessly uses other people for his own gain

W

wag (v) to move up and down or from side to side; **tongues wag** people are talking about someone else's behaviour

wearied (adj) very tired

weather-beaten (adj) with a face made brown and lined by the wind and sun

well-to-do (adj) rich

what not (n) an expression used at the end of a list of things when you do not want to give the names of everything

whereabouts (n) the place where someone or something is

whet (v) **whet someone's appetite** to increase someone's desire

whim (n) a sudden, unreasonable wish

wicked (adj) morally very wrong

widow (n) a woman whose husband has died and who has not married again

wig (n) false hair

wind (n) **the wind's in that quarter** that seems to be the situation

windowpane (n) a piece of glass in a window

wink (v) to close one eye as a sign of amusement

wire (v/n) to send a **telegram**

wireless (n) a radio

wisteria (n) a climbing plant with purple or white flowers

wistfully (adv) wishing for something that is unlikely to be true

wits (n pl) **frighten somebody out of their wits** to frighten somebody very much

worn out (adj) very tired

wrathful (adj) extremely angry

wrench (v) to pull hard and turn

wretched (adj) unhappy

wry (adj) showing a mixture of amusement and displeasure

Activities

The Mystery of Hunter's Lodge

Before you read

1   Look at these words from the story. Check the meaning of unfamiliar words
     in the Word List.

     bloodstain   *gruesome*   *influenza*   *lodge*   *moor*   *motive*
     nemesis   *revolver*   *vanish*   *wicked*

After you read: Understanding

2   Which of these people is:
     1 a murderer?   **2** a famous detective?   **3** a police officer?
     4 a murder victim?   **5** an actress?

     Hercule Poirot   Zoe Havering   Roger Havering
     Harrington Pace   Japp

3   What is the motive for the murder?

4   In what way is the housekeeper a mysterious figure?

After you read: Speaking

5   Work in pairs. Take the parts of Mr and Mrs Havering and recreate the
     conversation in which you plan the murder of Havering's uncle. Start like this:
     Mrs Havering: You're spending too much money. We can't continue like this.
     Mr Havering: But what can we do?

The Million Dollar Bond Robbery

Before you read

6 In this story, a bank employee is asked to accompany bonds worth a million dollars on their journey by ship from London to New York. When he arrives in New York, he does not have the bonds. How do you think the robbery took place?

After you read: Understanding

7 Are these statements true or false?

1 The bonds disappeared from the *Olympia*.
2 Mr Ridgeway is completely innocent.
3 The thief had a key to Mr Ridgeway's trunk.
4 The thief was on the *Olympia*.
5 The bonds were thrown into the sea.

8 What were the most important clues that allowed Poirot to solve the mystery?

After you read: Speaking

9 Explain what happened to the bonds from the moment they were counted in front of Mr Ridgeway.

The Adventure of the Clapham Cook

Before you read

10 Read these lines from the story.

"I want you to find my cook . . . Walked out of the house on Wednesday, without so much as a word to me, and never came back."

"I am sorry, Madame, but I do not touch this particular kind of business."

1 Why do you think Poirot is not interested in the case?
2 What can the client say to persuade him to take it?
3 How might the case become more interesting?

After you read: Understanding

11 Answer these questions.
   1 Why does the cook leave her place of employment?
   2 Who proves to be a thief?
   3 Who is murdered?
   4 Why does Poirot frame Mrs Todd's cheque?

After you read: Speaking

12 Tell the story from the point of view of either Mr Simpson or Mrs Todd.

Accident

Before you read

13 "A murderer is seldom content with one crime." How true do you think this is? Are some types of murderer more likely to murder again than others? What are the possible reasons for committing a number of murders?

After you read: Understanding

14 Whose words are these? Who is the speaker talking to? Who and what are they talking about?
   1 "I didn't say she was innocent. I said she was acquitted."
   2 "... I believe it was her idea originally. She didn't like my being so worried."
   3 "I'm afraid there's been the most dreadful accident ..."

After you read: Speaking

15 Discuss how the fortune-teller's prediction came true. How could Mr Evans have avoided his mistake?

The Lernean Hydra

Before you read

16 These words and phrases are important to the story. Check their meaning in the Word List.

arsenic   autopsy   dispensary   exhume   gastric ulcer   hydra   rumour   post-mortem

After you read: Understanding

17 How and why did Mrs Oldfield die? For what reasons can these people all be considered possible suspects in the murder case?

Dr Oldfield   Jean Moncrieffe   Nurse Harrison   Beatrice King

After you read: Speaking

18 Work in pairs. Imagine a conversation, immediately after the events in this story, between Nurse Harrison and Dr Oldfield.

Student A: You are Dr Oldfield. Ask questions to find out why your wife was murdered. Express your feelings towards Nurse Harrison.

Student B: You are Nurse Harrison. Answer Dr Oldfield's questions. Explain your feelings before, during and after the murder.

The Stymphalian Birds

Before you read

19 What does the crime of blackmail involve? (Check the Word List if you do not know the meaning of *blackmail*.) If you are being blackmailed, what are your options?

After you read: Understanding

20 Answer the following questions.

1 What do you think would have happened if Harold Waring had not met Hercule Poirot?

2 How do you think things change after their conversation?

21   What is the role of the Polish ladies in the story?

22   Which of the women in the story pretends to be a man?

After you read: Speaking

23   Explain how the two women blackmail Mr Waring.

Tape-Measure Murder

Before you read

24   In "Tape-Measure Murder" Miss Marple is an elderly woman who often solves murder mysteries in her own village. How do you think her methods of investigation will differ from Poirot's?

After you read: Understanding

25   Complete this chart.

Victim:	
Weapon:	
Murderer:	
Motive:	
Main clue:	

26   Look back at your answer to Activity 24. Were you correct?

After you read: Speaking

27   Imagine a newspaper interview after the crime is solved.
Student A: You are the reporter. Ask Miss Marple about the case and how she identified the murderer.
Student B: You are Miss Marple. Answer the reporter's questions.

Whole book

Writing

1   Explain the role of Captain Hastings in the Poirot stories. What does the relationship between Poirot and Hastings contribute to the stories?

2   In what way is "Accident" completely different from the other stories? How would Poirot have dealt with the same situation, do you think?

3   Compare the personalities and lifestyles of Miss Marple and Hercule Poirot.

4   Which is your favourite story in the collection? Explain why.

5   What do we learn from these stories about the period in which they take place?

6   Think of a famous writer of detective stories in the literature of your own country. In what ways are his/her stories similar to and different from those of Agatha Christie?